THE HIDDEN FOREST

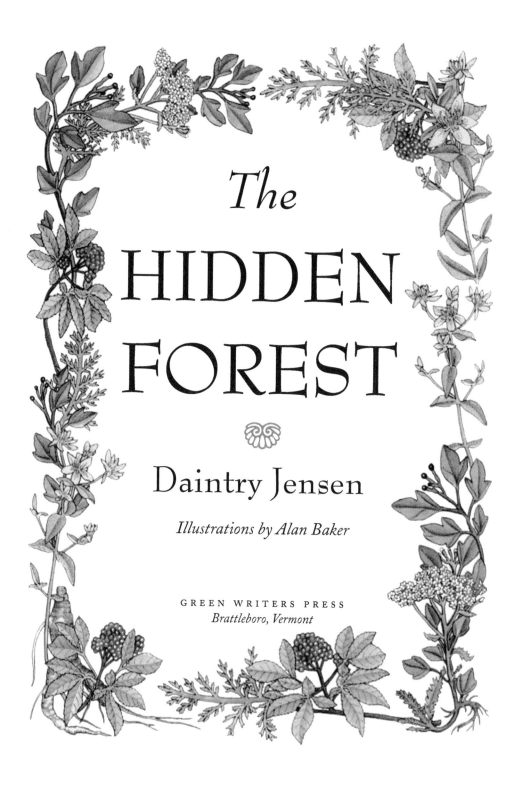

The
HIDDEN
FOREST

Daintry Jensen

Illustrations by Alan Baker

GREEN WRITERS PRESS
Brattleboro, Vermont

Printed in the United States

10 9 8 7 6 5 4 3 2 1

Green Writers Press is a Vermont-based publisher whose mission is to spread
a message of hope and renewal through the words and images we publish.
Throughout we will adhere to our commitment to preserving and protecting
the natural resources of the earth. To that end, a percentage of our proceeds will
be donated to environmental activist groups. Green Writers Press gratefully
acknowledges support from individual donors, friends, and readers to help
support the environment and our publishing initiative.

Giving Voice to Writers & Artists Who will Make the World a Better Place
Green Writers Press | Brattleboro, Vermont
www.greenwriterspress.com

Visit the author's website at:
www.daintryjensen.com

ISBN: 978-0-9909733-4-8

PRINTED ON PAPER WITH PULP THAT COMES FROM FSC-CERTIFIED FORESTS, MANAGED FORESTS THAT
GUARANTEE RESPONSIBLE ENVIRONMENTAL, SOCIAL, AND ECONOMIC PRACTICES BY LIGHTNING SOURCE
ALL WOOD PRODUCT COMPONENTS USED IN BLACK & WHITE, STANDARD COLOR, OR SELECT COLOR
PAPERBACK BOOKS, UTILIZING EITHER CREAM OR WHITE BOOKBLOCK PAPER, THAT ARE
MANUFACTURED IN THE LAVERGNE, TENNESSEE PRODUCTION CENTER ARE
SUSTAINABLE FORESTRY INITIATIVE® (SFI®) CERTIFIED SOURCING

To Mom and Dad,

For opening the door to this magical, faraway place
that's always nearby
and for giving us the freedom to truly explore,
with much love and gratitude.

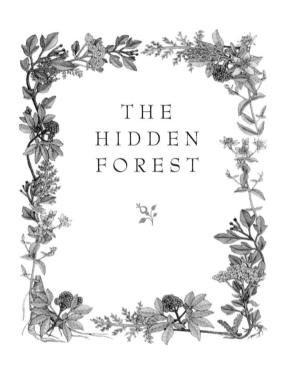

THE
HIDDEN
FOREST

Chapter 1

ANYWHERE
BUT HERE

ADELAIDE awoke with a start and looked around her shadowy bedroom, trying to get oriented. It was the middle of the night, and she'd had a nightmare again, but not the usual kind. There were no monsters trying to get her, no cliffs she was falling from. It was quite the opposite. It was that her father was still alive and they were planning to go on a hike and an adventure together, just the two of them. But that couldn't be, she thought as she lay back on her pillow, staring into the blackness. Her father had died almost a year ago. Now it was just her mother, her younger brother Louis, and last but definitely not least, Dash, their Jack Russell terrier.

Adelaide lay in her four poster bed, thinking. She grabbed her explorer's head lamp hanging from one of the bedposts, put it on, and flicked on the high beam. Adelaide looked like a fairly normal girl of twelve years old, but she wasn't. Blond hair, blue eyes, and a love of blueberry pie would put her right in the mix, but really she loved anything that was different. Adelaide hated the ordinary. All she wanted was to be grown-up and become the world-famous explorer she knew she was deep down inside and go off in search of the extraordinary. There was *so much* to do and see that her time as a kid was just being *wasted*, she thought as she stared at the posters of exotic places on her walls. There was one of the Great Pyramid of Giza in Egypt, and who could resist the map of the lost city of the Incas, Machu Picchu, in Peru?

She looked over at the aerial photograph of Howland Island in the Pacific Ocean, close to where Amelia Earhart disappeared during her solo flight around the world. How brave she was, Adelaide thought as she reached for her dog-eared biography of Amelia. She didn't open it, just held on to it, something she loved to do at night, when it was dark and she felt all alone. Someday she'd follow in her footsteps—she'd make sure of it, Adelaide thought as she drifted off to sleep.

Chapter 2

CHANCE

"ADDY, have you finished packing for Nantucket? You need to help your brother too!" Adelaide's eyes flew open when she heard her mother's voice. Her neck was stiff from falling asleep with the head lamp on.

"Oops," Adelaide said as she slipped it off and turned off the high beam. She looked over at the map of Nantucket Island on her wall next to the poster of the Great Pyramid of Giza. Nantucket looked so small and flat.

"Not exactly Kilimanjaro," she mumbled as she hopped off her bed and grabbed the pair of binoculars that she kept on her bedside table. She opened the window and looked through them down into the backyard where Louis was playing catch with Dash. She adjusted the focus and couldn't help but laugh when the tennis ball bounced off the dog's head and into the bushes.

"Outstanding," she shouted down to her brother.

"Dash loves it. Come down and see," Louis shouted back. He was four years younger but he liked to pretend they were the same age.

"Kid stuff. Besides, Mom said you're supposed to be packing for Nantucket."

"Are you?" Louis asked, grinning because he knew she wasn't.

"None of your business," she said as she closed the window. She didn't want to go. There weren't any pyramids on Nantucket as far as she knew. What was she going to do there, staying with her grandparents? It was just another ploy of her mother's to shuffle them off. Who could blame her really? Adelaide thought. A sadness clung to their home like the kind of dampness that's only in the British Isles. At least that's what Adelaide overheard her aunt Julie say to her mother one night when she and Louis were hiding on the back staircase eavesdropping. It was true. Adelaide felt it every time she walked by her dad's empty study. It left a terrible pit in her stomach, until she started avoiding it altogether and took the back staircase whenever she went up to her bedroom. Maybe it would be good to get away.

Adelaide opened her closet door, and there, hanging on the hook, was the leather flight jacket her dad had given her, just like Amelia's. She looked past it and started rifling through her closet. She pulled out the metal detector her grandfather Poppa had surprised her with last Christmas. Maybe there were some buried treasures from shipwrecks she could look for at least. She grabbed some snorkeling gear too.

"Now we're getting somewhere," she said as she started to pile up the gear to take. The bedroom door opened, and her mother popped her head in.

"Adelaide, why didn't you answer me—" She stopped mid-sentence when she saw the pile of stuff on Adelaide's floor. "Oh, sweetie . . ."

"Mother, please. These mere trinkets are absolutely necessary for the journey we're about to embark on."

"You don't mean you want to take all this junk with you?"

"I would hardly call my equipment junk. It's of the utmost importance. Now, maps, where are my maps?"

Adelaide went over to the wall and carefully took down the map of Nantucket. "I think I might need this one too," she said as she took down the map of the internal walkways of the Pyramid of Giza. "There may be some universal symbology that could be of use in the days to come."

"The days to come?" her mother asked as she started taking out some of Adelaide's summer clothes to pack.

"Yes, and Mom," Adelaide said as she came over and rested a hand on her mother's shoulder. "I'm sorry I won't be here to look after you. Will you be all right?"

"I'll be okay. I'll have Dash with me. Nantucket with Nana and Poppa is really the best place for you guys this summer," her mother said, trying to smile. It didn't fool Adelaide. Everyone said that in time things would start to get better, but Adelaide was starting to wonder. Things didn't feel any better yet, and all she could think about was tomorrow and tomorrow and tomorrow. Because tomorrow, maybe there would be some adventure to undertake, pyramids to climb, secret passages to explore, and the promise of the future to help forget the past.

"Rein it in while you're there, okay? Mind your grandparents," her mom was saying. "And most important, take care of your brother. What time is it? Go call him, will you? The ferry leaves in a few hours, and we've got to get you guys packed up."

Adelaide opened the window again and shouted down to him, "Louis! Come up and pack! Pronto!"

"Addy, you know I hate all that shouting. Go down and tell him. And you can take one piece of equipment with you, but only one."

After her mother left, Adelaide checked the hallway to make sure the coast was clear, then tucked the snorkeling gear into the back of her duffel bag along with her binoculars. She put some clothes on top to hide them and put the metal detector over by the bag. Then she thought a moment and, opening the closet door, looked at the flight jacket. She carefully took it down, folded it, and put it into the duffel bag.

"Most excellent," she said as she surveyed it all.

Chapter 3

STRANGE TIDINGS

ADELAIDE, Louis, and their mom arrived at the dock just as the ferry was blowing its horn. Adelaide knew this was the moment to show she was grown-up, but it was hard to keep the tears from pricking her eyes as she faced her mom to say good-bye.

"You guys have to go. Listen, you're going to have a great time," her mom said as she gave Louis his baseball glove.

The ferry blew its horn again, and Adelaide and Louis gave their mom one more kiss. They boarded the ferry and went up to the top deck to wave good-bye. Adelaide put on her big black sunglasses and stood an arm's length away from Louis so people wouldn't think they were related.

The ferry slowly backed out into the harbor and turned around as it headed into the wind and the vast Atlantic Ocean ahead of them. She was getting excited thinking about exploring the island. . . even if her younger brother was in tow. She sighed and looked over at Louis, who was talking to himself in a troll voice and cracking up.

"Louis, *what* are you doing?"

"Oh, nothing," he said, when all of a sudden a seagull swooped down, landed right between them, and let out a loud *squaawk!*

"Hey, look at him," said Louis. The seagull moved its head just like Louis did, almost as if it were imitating him.

"Hey," said Louis. He took a step to the right, and the seagull followed suit. "He's copying me!"

"What's going on?" Adelaide laughed.

Louis went around in a circle, and the seagull did the same. Adelaide and Louis were both laughing now; Adelaide couldn't help herself. The seagull squawked again. It was acting almost like a person. And then the strangest thing happened: as Louis watched, the seagull winked at him and flew away.

"Hey!" Louis called after him. "Don't go!" He looked at Adelaide. "He just winked at me."

"Come on, Louis, seagulls don't wink. Do they?" She looked after it as it circled the ferry twice, staring at them, and with one last *squaaawk* flew out ahead of the boat and grew smaller and smaller until it was a speck on the horizon.

"Do you think he's going all the way to Nantucket?"

"I don't know. It's conceivable, I suppose," said Adelaide.

"Incon*thiev*able!" Louis exclaimed. Adelaide stared at him. "Don't you remember? The little guy in that movie about the princess?" He laughed. "He was awesome."

"Kid stuff," Adelaide said as she looked out to sea. It was going to be a long rest of the summer, she thought. They watched the sea for a long time, looking for the seagull to come back, but it was gone.

"Look!" Adelaide said after some time had passed. "There's the island, I think. Yes, it is!" They both watched in silence a moment as the Great Point Lighthouse came into view, very tall and white, with a black top. It always stood out against the vast blueness of the Atlantic Ocean.

"I think I can smell Nana's Portuguese toast with homemade blueberry jam on it," Louis shouted to no one in particular.

"Yeah? Well, I think I can *taste* her homemade blueberry ice cream that's just starting to melt on the cone," shouted Adelaide.

"Yum!" shouted Louis.

They had to admit, they loved all these things about visiting their grandparents, who lived out in a wild part of the island called Polpis. There was lots of uncharted territory to investigate. They were told they could go anywhere they wanted, except past the stone wall that was beyond Nana's vegetable garden. That was a standing rule.

As the ferry pulled into Nantucket Harbor and up to the dock, they could pick out their grandparents immediately in the crowd. Poppa had on a blue and white striped golf hat and a pipe hanging out of his mouth, and Nana wore her old straw hat covered in rumpled silk flowers. Nana smiled when she saw them, and Adelaide couldn't help but smile back.

Chapter 4

THE MERQUEEN'S ROSE

ADELAIDE and Louis had only been on Nantucket a few days when Louis started sniffling. Nana thought it would be best for him to stay in his room for the afternoon and rest so he could nip a possible summer cold in the bud. She was on her way out to play golf with the Holy Rollers, a foursome of her friends that she had nicknamed because they liked to get together and play poker at the church on Saturday nights. Adelaide wanted to go with her, but Nana said it would be more fun for her another time, when it wasn't such a serious golf game. "And remember," she said, "stay on our side of the stone wall. There are some loose stones on it, and I don't want you getting hurt." Poppa was to stay home and keep an eye on things, but as soon as Nana left, he promptly fell asleep under the green umbrella on the porch, his golf hat covering his eyes.

Adelaide felt restless. She wanted to go on an adventure, but she knew she wasn't to go past the stone wall. All of these rules, she thought. Hadn't she heard somewhere that rules were made to be broken? She was sure she had. She went to her room, grabbed her binoculars, and flew out the back door into the summer breeze. She climbed up into the old oak tree by the house, sat in the crook of some branches, and looked through her binoculars to get the lay of the land. Wildflowers were in bloom all around Nana's vegetable garden. It was all so inviting! She decided to gather a bunch of wildflowers and start documenting the flora and fauna on the island. She hopped out of the tree, grabbed an old basket and some garden shears that were hanging on the fence surrounding the vegetable garden, and began looking around.

She reached the stone wall where so many of the flowers were growing when something over the wall grabbed her attention—a beautiful white rose. It was larger than the rest of the roses on the bush and looked almost too perfect. Ooh, she had to get that one. She looked back to see if Poppa was still asleep. He was. She didn't even have to see him—she could hear his snoring all the way from the porch. She looked back at the stone wall. It looked harmless. Who was to know if she quickly climbed over it?

Adelaide looked this way and that, then scrambled over the wall. There, that wasn't so hard. She went over to the rose and smelled it. As she clipped it she decided it would go right in the center of her notebook, when something else caught her eye—a flash of movement and light by the grove of birch trees. Something was over there. She stepped closer. Nothing. Then, a flash—there it was again! Now over in the middle of the grove. Flash, flash! Then she saw something, under a fern leaf, sparkling in the sunlight.

"Hello," she whispered. "Hello? Is anyone there?" She looked through her binoculars.

"Psst!" a voice whispered back. She inched closer. "Psssssst! Hey you!" it whispered again.

To her astonishment, a tiny brown and tan field mouse stepped out from underneath the fern. He wore a gold helmet with a red ruby sparkling in the center. He looked nervously about as his paw gripped a tiny gold sword in a hammered, bejeweled belt.

"Listen," he said, "I'm not supposed to be talking to you humans. But . . . she'd be really mad if she knew you took her rose. You better put it back and go on your merry way, got it?"

Adelaide stared at the creature in shock. She had never seen a mouse talk before, although she'd always believed that animals *could* talk—they just didn't bother to do it around people.

"Look. C'mere. A little closer," the mouse said. Adelaide knelt down. "Okay. Now, you know about the merqueen, don'tcha?" the mouse asked.

"The mer-queen?" Adelaide repeated. "No, I don't think so. I'm familiar with mermaids though. My Poppa has told me stories—"

"Well, this ain't no fairy tale, lady," the mouse said, cutting her off. "There's a queen, see, and she's a mermaid, like, but she's *the* mermaid—the queen of all underwater creatures. Even the merking gets the lead out when she's around."

"But why? Is she really evil, or—"

"Shh! I can't go into it! You just have no idea," said the mouse as he wiped a tear from his eye and tried not to shake.

"Well, I'm really sorry, Mr. . . . uh, Mr. . . . "

"Oh yes, of course, of course, of course. We should introduce ourselves, you're right, of course." With one sweeping gesture, he removed his helmet and bowed very low. "My name is Captain Henry the Twenty-Sixth. I am pleased to make your acquaintance."

"Well, thank you, Captain Henry. My name is Adelaide, and I didn't know the rose belonged to anyone, so I'm sorry. And I'm not a grown-up yet, although I tell you, I can't wait until I am."

"You're not?" he asked as he stepped forward and sniffed at her. "Ah, jeez. Well, it's impossible to tell with you humans, you all look alike. Anyway, you'd better beat it, and I mean, like, yesterday. She's got watchers all over the place keeping an eye out." He put on his helmet and glanced around one more time.

"And if I was you, I'd put the rose back, like, *yesterday*, got it?" he said. Adelaide nodded, eyes wide.

"Good," the mouse said, adjusting his helmet just so. "All right, little lady, ciao for now." And with a flash, Captain Henry the Twenty-Sixth was gone.

Adelaide spun around looking for his gold helmet, but she couldn't see him anywhere.

She sighed and wished he had stayed longer so she could ask him questions. Who was the mer-queen? What did she look like? Was there any way to go spy on her? Where did she live, and was she really as mean as Captain Henry had made her sound?

She looked down at the rose in her basket. What should she do? There was no way to put it back really, because she'd already clipped it. Maybe she could keep it and just leave a note for the mer-queen explaining what had happened. Adelaide decided that's what she would do, so she picked up her basket of flowers and went to Nana's gardening shack, where she found an old brown pencil and a piece of paper. She thought for a moment before writing.

Dear Your Highness, the Merqueen,

I am so sorry for having clipped your rose, but, you see, I didn't know it belonged to anyone. Usually wildflowers are really, well, independent and don't belong to anyone. Hence the term "wild." But I digress! After I clipped it, I couldn't see any way to put it back! So I've decided to take it into my Nana's house and put it in water, so it doesn't die such an early death. So if you need it, that's where it'll be. Thank you very much. Have an OUTSTANDING day.

Adelaide

There, that should do it. So it wasn't like she was stealing the rose, she was really *saving* the rose, and letting the merqueen know where it was. She put the note where the rose had been and scrambled back over the wall. She made one last scan across the horizon through her binoculars, then ran back to the house to tell Louis all about Captain Henry and the merqueen.

Chapter 5

THE SANKATY LYNX

LOUIS awoke to the sound of scratching on the metal screen door on the far side of his room. He started. Was he having a nightmare? But no, it was still after-noon. That's right—he had a cold and had been taking a nap. Maybe he had become delirious. Maybe he had delirium and was going to die! He had read about delirium in one of his war books, and he remembered it had killed many men.

Suddenly the bedroom door opened and Adelaide came bounding in, giving Louis another start.

"Hey, don't you know how to knock or any-thing? I was just—"

Adelaide, who was out of breath, cut him off, she was so eager to tell him her news. "Louis, you won't believe what just happened to me!" she said.

"What?" Louis asked, when there was another loud scratch at the screen door.

They looked at each other, eyes wide. Adelaide knew that Nana wouldn't be home for another hour or two and Poppa was still asleep. Plus, the scratching sounded like it came from down low on the door, so unless it was a very small person, it must be—something else.

Scratch, scratch, scratch. It was even louder now and more fervent.

"Well," said Louis, "aren't you going to open that?"

"Me?"

"That's right, oh queen of the great explorers."

"Okay, okay! Where's that shield you got for your birthday last summer?"

"It's plastic!" he said as took it from the closet.

"It's better than—" *Scratch. SCRATCH, SCRATCH.*

Adelaide grabbed the shield. "Here goes," she said as she slowly opened the screen door, which led out to the backyard.

There stood an animal that looked like a cat,

but a very large one with long black tufts shooting out of its ears. Not only that, but it had on a tweed vest with a green cravat tied around its neck.

"My dear Miss Adelaide, forgive the intrusion," the creature said with a slight English accent. He bowed. Louis gasped. "Master Louis, good afternoon. It's a delight to make your acquaintance."

"You can talk, too!" Adelaide burst out. "Just like Captain Henry!"

"Well, I wouldn't say just like, exactly. Captain Henry the Twenty-Sixth comes from the, shall we say, south side of the island. They have a different way of doing and saying things down there, my dear."

"I see," said Adelaide, not sure if she should believe what she was seeing and hearing. "Are you a cat—a wild cat?"

The creature gasped. "My dear, you cut me to the quick! Thank the heavens my dear mother was not around to hear that," he said as he took out a handkerchief from his vest pocket and gingerly patted his brow. "No, no, it's all right. I know you don't know about all that exists in the Hidden Forest. My name is Max and I am a lynx, my dear, a Sankaty lynx to be exact. We are a very noble breed indeed."

By now Louis had begun to recover and moved a little closer to the lynx.

"It's all right, little boy. I won't eat you. Little boys are especially unappetizing—all that dirt. Smoked bluefish and caviar is really the only way to go on Nantucket, don't you think?"

"I like bluefish!" said Louis.

"Adelaide! Louis!" called Poppa, who had woken up from his nap.

"Ah, yes. Well, to delay no further, I've come for the rose. The merqueen's rose. I don't feel very strongly about it, you understand, but the merqueen could cause some very serious problems if she found out that it was nicked. By a girl, nonetheless. With two legs. She's always wanted legs, you see, from the very beginning."

"Oh no!" Adelaide said, starting to feel a hollow pit in her stomach. "So then, you work for the merqueen?" she asked, starting to back away and taking Louis with her. The lynx let out another gasp.

"Heavens, no, my dear. We lynx just like to keep the peace on the island."

"Captain Henry told me that it might be a problem, but I couldn't think of how to put it back, since I had already clipped it. I'm so sorry. I shouldn't have gone over the stone wall, like Nana told us," said Adelaide. Maybe grown-ups did know a thing or two after all.

"Quite right," Max said, eyeing her, almost as if he could read her mind. "But I'll let you in on a little secret about Nantucket roses. There's something quite magical about them, you know. I do believe they have more than one life in them."

"Adelaide and Louis! Let's go fishing!" they heard Poppa shout.

"That's our grandfather, Mr. Lynx. I'm so sorry about the rose. Here it is. If you can put it back, I'd be so grateful."

"Call me Max, my dear." He grimaced. "My Lord, how loudly men walk. As if Neptune himself had legs. I'll hurry," he told Adelaide, "but I'm not sure it's going to be enough for her. She can be rather *touchy* about some things. You know how queens are; we'll just have to see." He took the rose very carefully in his mouth. "I'll be in touch. Cheerio," he added, and winked at them. Then he quickly leapt out the door and was across the yard before they knew it. All very silently and beautifully, thought Adelaide as she watched him go.

Poppa appeared at the bedroom door. "Well, well. Up to no good I see," he teased.

"Poppa, what's that on your lip?" asked Adelaide

as she saw a blue glob of something that looked suspiciously like blueberry pie.

"Hmm? Oh, just testing Nana's pie, making sure it wasn't *poisoned*. Us commoners sometimes have to do that for the queen, you know," he said as he wiped the side of his mouth.

"The merqueen?!" asked Louis.

"Shh," Adelaide said quickly. "Are we going fishing now?" she asked Poppa.

"Hmm . . . yes, yes, fishing. Onward. No self-indulgent navel gazing for the likes of us. Your Nana has always said that only leads to weakness, and I'd have to agree."

He started out for the shed. Adelaide pulled Louis aside and said, "I don't think we should say anything to Nana or Poppa about all that's happened. Something tells me they might not understand."

"Okay. But what if the merqueen, whoever that is, gets mad about the rose and sends, like, a *giant lobster*, or worse, a *huuuge squid* with ten thousand tentacles to come get—"

"Shhhh, calm down. That's not going to happen. Besides, I met a real captain today. Captain Henry the Twenty-Sixth. He has a gold sword and everything."

"Is he a lynx too?"

"Not exactly. No, he's more like, well . . . he's sort of a mouse," Adelaide said, trying to be reassuring.

"A *mouse*? Oh yeah, he'll really help defend us against a *giant squid* with ten thousand tentacles."

"You need to calm down, Louis. I mean it."

"I think I have delirium," Louis said, starting to sit down.

"You don't have delirium. You're just getting carried away as usual. Just think about Nana's blueberry pie and you'll be fine," Adelaide said as she took his arm and started to lead the way out.

"Yeah. Oh yeah. I love that pie."

"And you're not going to get it if you're freaking out," Adelaide reminded him.

"You're right. Okay, let's go fishing," he said, trying to smile but not quite able to.

"Right, fishing." Adelaide said. But she had started to have heart palpitations whenever she thought about clipping that rose.

Chapter 6

AWAKENING THE QUEEN

IN the deepest and darkest of underwater caves, the merqueen was sleeping on a giant gold and bejeweled scallop shell when she jolted awake. She was quite a beautiful creature, with violet eyes that glowed in the darkness and long, silvery, emerald-green hair that was adorned with strands of pearls and emerald seahorse medallions.

"Something's been...disturbed," she murmured. "Loud mouth frogs, come here at once!"

In hopped two of her minions, the loud mouth frogs. These were not the normal garden-variety frog. They were very large and slimy black with long, blood-red tongues. They wore green vests made of seaweed with tiny freshwater pearls sewn around the collar.

"Your Highneth," one lisped, and made a deep bow.

"Get up, you fool, and listen to me. I've just felt something quite out of the ordinary, and I don't like it one bit. Something quite, quite . . . "

"A girl, Your Majesty!" the other frog said.

"A girl?"

"A human girl, to be exact," said the first frog. "With two legth and all that."

"Two legs, you say?" the merqueen asked as her violet eyes glowed brighter.

"Yes! And she has just abthconded with the rothe, my queen," the frog lisped, with fear in his eyes.

True to form, the merqueen's violet eyes glowed with a most malevolent light as she gazed upon the two informants.

"My rose?! No one would dare touch it! If you're lying to me . . . ," she started as she eyed them.

"Oh no, my prethous queen," the first one said with a gasp.

"Never!" the second frog insisted.

"Hmm. Smells fishy to me," whispered the merqueen.

Before the two loud mouth frogs had time to look at each other with their bulging red eyes, there was a huge bolt of lightning and a fiery blast. Then silence, and it was as if they had never been there at all, except for an errant froggy toe here and a leftover froggy eyeball there.

"There, that's better," said the merqueen as she smoothed down her emerald hair. "I do hate liars so." But she didn't look relieved, and her violet eyes dimmed. If anyone had so much as touched her rose, oh, how they would sorely regret it. "Especially some human girl with two legs. Unless...," the merqueen murmured to herself, then paused, thinking. Slowly, she smiled, for the first time in ages.

Chapter 7

DIGGING DEEPER

"HOLD this," said Poppa when they got to the shed, handing Adelaide the tackle box, which made her jump back and bump her head on the shelf that held all the fishing rods.

"It doesn't bite, you know," said Poppa, laughing.

This is crazy, Adelaide thought. She hated being so jumpy. This isn't the way Amelia Earhart would be acting. She needed more information; she needed to get to the bottom of who this merqueen was. Then she'd know what she was up against.

As Poppa rummaged through the shed and got out the fishing rods, Adelaide thought of a plan. Maybe they could stop by the Atheneum, which was the library in town. She and Louis could say they were looking for summer books on their reading list, but they could really go in search of mer-queen lore.

"Poppa, maybe we should go out to the wharf and fish off the docks *in town*."

"The docks?" Poppa asked.

"Yeah, didn't you say that was one of your favorite things to do growing up?" Adelaide said, hoping beyond hope that he actually had.

"Oh yes. My favorite, actually."

The docks turned out to be the perfect place for them. There was no wind, so it was warm and pleasant as they waited and waited and *waited* to catch a fish. Adelaide was getting nervous that they would run out of time to go to the Atheneum before it closed. Finally Louis had a bite on the end of his line, and he slowly reeled in a lovely. . . eel.

"Ugh," said Adelaide.

"What do you mean?" said Poppa. "Eel's delicious!"

"Scrumptious!" said Louis, laughing.

"Hey, Poppa, do you think we might have time for a little stop on the way home?" Adelaide asked, starting to gather up all their gear.

Poppa pulled up outside the Atheneum, and Adelaide and Louis ran up the stairs to the grand entryway. They came into the central reading room, which was huge, with book-lined shelves that almost reached the ceiling. The Atheneum had a musty smell that made Adelaide feel like an adventure was about to begin. What a cool place. She looked around, not knowing where to start, when she saw the information counter and headed over to it.

"Excuse me," Adelaide said to the bespectacled librarian behind the counter. "I'm looking for some, uh, information!"

"Join the club," said the librarian, who looked like she was almost drowning in returned books.

"I need to look up—" Adelaide began.

"Google. Second floor. You need a computer, dear, not my feeble brain."

Google, of course. There had to be something on one of the search engines about the merqueen.

"Thanks," Adelaide said, and turned, looking for Louis, but he was nowhere to be seen. She went around the corner and saw a large room that was wall-to-wall maps of every shape and size. Louis stood at the doorway, taking it all in.

"Wow, how cool is this?" Adelaide exclaimed. They went in and looked around the room. The maps were old, and many included illustrations of sea monsters and paintings of great ships. There were some of the Americas, Africa, and India as well as of Nantucket. It seemed as if every corner of the world was represented on these walls.

"Okay, I just found my new favorite place ever," Adelaide said as she pored over the maps, taking in every detail.

"There you are," said Poppa, standing at the door. "Ready?"

"Just give us two minutes, okay?" said Adelaide.

"I'll give you four, but then we've got to get home, righty-O?"

Adelaide ran up to the second floor with Louis close behind. She found an empty cubicle with a computer and looked around to make sure no one was watching. She typed "merqueen" into the search engine and started reading.

"Uh-oh," Adelaide said as she scanned the results.

"What?" Louis asked.

"'Merqueen: Queen of the half-human underwater creatures and beyond. Half-woman, half-fish creature. Ancient mariners' tales speak of these visitors from the sea, who are said to be beautiful, strong, seductive, and dangerous, just like the sea itself. Some can be quite evil but clever, passionate but vain. Given to fits of fury that can cause tremendous upheaval unlike anything one might have experienced before in its breadth and brutality...'"

"Holy—" Louis started.

"There's more," Adelaide continued. "The queen is said to be the most powerful of all merpeople and not to be provoked or dire circumstances could prevail." Adelaide gulped and looked at Louis. "This is a fiasco!"

"Well, don't look at me. You're the one who took that stupid rose in the first place."

"Thanks, Louis," she said as she clicked off the computer. "Come on, Poppa's waiting. And remember, not a word of this to anyone," she said as she led the way out.

"Right, merqueen's the word—I mean mum's the word," Louis said as they made their way down the stairs.

Chapter 8

JOINING THE CLUB

POPPA, Adelaide, and Louis pulled up to their house just in time to see Nana taking her golf bag out of the car.

"She should know better than to do that," said Poppa as he got out of the car. Adelaide went over to help, but Nana brushed her away with a wave of her hand.

"I don't need a caddy, Adelaide. I'm not that old and decrepit. Not yet."

"I wish you'd let me play," Adelaide said as she took the Big Bertha driver out of the bag and pretended to hit a golf ball.

"You know you're not old enough. Someday, don't worry," Nana said.

"Someday might be too late," Adelaide murmured as Louis came running up with the dead eel swinging from his fishing line.

"Isn't it beautific!" he said, looking at the eel like it was true love.

"Absolutely gorgeous," Nana said, winking at Poppa. "Eel is just so delicious. Add an island salad and it's perfection. Adelaide, why don't you go into the vegetable garden and get some lettuce?" Adelaide looked over at the garden and the stone wall beyond it apprehensively.

"There are clippers by the shed," Nana said over her shoulder as she went into the house. The sun was starting to set, and it was getting darker. Adelaide kept her eye out as she went over by the garden shed and grabbed the clippers. She looked around the garden, saw a head of lettuce that looked about right, and bent down to clip it.

"Excellent choice."

She jumped back, and there, sitting quietly in the shadows watching her, was Max, the Sankaty lynx.

"Max!"

"My dear, you seem quite on edge."

"Oh, Max, we went to the Atheneum today and I made some inquiries about the merqueen."

"Ah. And now you're feeling, shall we say, some-what apprehensive."

"Very apprehensive," Adelaide sighed as she clipped the lettuce.

"Well," Max said, "I have a thought that might be of help. Fancy a little adventure to take your mind off things? And who knows, you might learn a thing or two along the way. After all, it's going to be a full moon tonight, and you know what that means."

"What?" asked Adelaide.

"Why, midnight golf, of course. Are you game?"

"Oh yes! I mean, I don't know," Adelaide hesitated as she glanced over at the stone wall.

"I wouldn't worry if I were you," Max said as he watched the early-evening light cast shadows across the stone wall.

"But what if Nana wakes up and I'm not there?"

"My dear Adelaide, in the Hidden Forest we're on a slightly different schedule," Max said, and Adelaide smiled back.

"Now, this is what you're to do," said Max, and he explained to her how the rest of the evening would go.

Chapter 9

MIDNIGHT GOLF

THAT night Adelaide was so excited about midnight golf, she didn't know how she was going to wait until the appointed hour. She decided to keep her clothes on under her nightgown so she'd be ready—for what, she didn't know. She knew she couldn't fall asleep, but she wanted Louis to, so she read out loud to him for a long time so he'd be good and tired when she turned out the light. It was very dark in the room, and all she could hear was the *tick tick tick* of the clock. Soon she could hear Louis snoring. "What a racket," she said out loud without meaning to.

"You can say that again," said a tiny voice.

Adelaide jumped up in her bed. Peering up at her from the floor were two beady eyes belonging to a tiny mouse wearing a silver helmet.

"Captain Henry?" she asked. "Is that you?"

"Where, where?" The mouse scrambled up onto the bed and ran behind Adelaide as he tried to get his tiny sword out of its sheath. "These darn things are made off island, and it sure does show."

"Wait, you're not Captain Henry."

"Me?" The mouse laughed. "You had me worried there for a second, had me scared. Captain Henry, he's not on our side anymore, didn't you hear?"

"He's not? What happened to him?" Adelaide asked, getting that pit in the bottom of her stomach again.

"Something too horrible to even put into words," the mouse whispered, looking around nervously. "But here I am, forgetting myself. You ever have that? Where you start doing one thing and then minutes later you're doing something else?"

"Well, sometimes I guess."

"For me it happens all the time. Like just the other day—" He sat down on her knee a moment, then stopped himself. "My stars, I'm doing it again. Look, you've got to stop me next time, or we'll be here all night. Now," he said, jumping up and adjusting his helmet, "I've been sent by Max to get you for the big game. Think you're up for it?"

"I can't wait," said Adelaide.

"Then onward, my little chickadee. After you, I insist." He bowed and motioned with his paw for her to lead the way. Adelaide quickly peeled her nightgown off of her sweatshirt and jeans. She grabbed her sneakers and head lamp, which she had hidden under the bed, and opened the screen door very quietly. With the mouse following close behind, Adelaide led the way out into the moonlit night.

They hadn't gotten very far when Adelaide started asking questions of her guide. How would they be able to play in the dark? What would she use for clubs? Who was going to be there? The mouse seemed slightly flustered by the barrage.

"Look, girlie, I'm just following orders, which are to guide you to the right place. It's all supposed to be part of the adventure anyway."

"Well, won't you even tell me your name, then?" asked Adelaide.

"Haven't I introduced myself? I could have sworn I had. My name's . . . my name's . . . wait, what is my name?"

"Do you at least remember where we're supposed to be going?"

"Oh sure, know it like the back of my hand. Hey! I remember now. My name's Pipsqueak. Lieutenant Pipsqueak, that is." He saluted her.

"Well, Lieutenant Pipsqueak, I'm Adelaide, and I want to thank you for showing me the way."

"My pleasure, Adelaide. And it's really Max who will be showing you the way. I'm just here to guide you tonight. And you can just call me Pipsqueak, okey-dokey? It won't be too long now."

They walked along in silence as Adelaide took in the sights. The moon, just coming out from behind some clouds, was very bright. They were going through a fairly dense and misty part of the forest behind Nana and Poppa's house, and Adelaide was feeling a little scared, even though it was very beautiful.

"How much longer, do you think?" she asked Pipsqueak.

"Oh, I'd say three shakes of a mouse's tail," he said as he pulled aside a branch. He led the way through, and Adelaide followed.

The forest mist soon gave way to a huge clearing where dozens of animals were gathered. Fireflies floated in clusters all around and

MAX, THE SANKATY LYNX, AT MIDNIGHT GOLF.

gave off a lovely dusky light. Just enough light to see a golf ball, thought Adelaide. She saw Max approaching, carrying his clubs as well as an extra set.

"Miss Adelaide, you've finally made it. Well done," he said as he handed her a set of golf clubs.

Adelaide couldn't believe what she was seeing. "Who are all these animals?" she asked Max.

"Oh, friends of mine, and hopefully soon to be friends of yours too," he said as he gave her an affectionate nudge with his muzzle.

The animals began to gather around her. They seemed to be grouped in teams, and one animal in each team carried clubs. There was a group of cats—regular house cats with collars and tags—and one of them carried a set of bright pink clubs just its size. This cat was slightly larger than the rest and had on a green plaid beret with a pompom on top.

"That's Fredrick," said Max. "He's from Scotland."

As if Fredrick had overheard Max, he took off his beret and bowed to Adelaide. "Top of the evening to you, my dear." Adelaide smiled at him.

The thing that struck Adelaide most was that all the animals were standing on their hind legs.

"Wow, look at them all!" she exclaimed.

"Oh yes," said Max. "We can all walk on our hind legs when needed, but it's much more comfortable to walk on all four. That doesn't help one's golf swing too much, however."

Adelaide saw a group of very bright red cardinals hopping about on the ground, one of which was carrying a lovely, tiny blue and white striped golf bag. There was also a group of golden retrievers who were practicing walking on their hind legs.

"But how, if you all have different-sized clubs, can you play together?" asked Adelaide.

"Ah. Well, in the Hidden Forest, once you decide on something and intend it to be so, it is. With a lot of concentration, to be sure, but intention is the key. We decided many moons ago that it would be much more of an adventure if we played golf under a full moon. So we all got together and made it so."

"And?" asked Adelaide.

"See for yourself," said Max, turning her to face all the animals. "Everyone ready?"

"Yup!"

"Yo!"

"Righty yo ho ho, over here!"

"Paws up, Max!"

"Now, we're going to close our eyes and spin around in a circle, and whoever can do it longest goes first."

Adelaide watched them all spin around and around and start bumping into one another, laughing. Finally, it was the cardinals who won out.

"Chirp, chirp, hooray!" they chirped.

"But Max, isn't the golf ball too big for them?"

"Just watch," he said.

Adelaide watched as the first cardinal went up to the first tee and teed up his ball. Right before Adelaide's eyes, the ball shrank to the size that was perfect for the bird. He held the club in his beak and swung. The golf ball went flying up into the air, through the sparkling fireflies, and out into the night. Everyone clapped and cheered.

"We're all for each other, you see," said Max. "There really isn't any such thing as competition among us."

"But that's so different from how Nana and Poppa play. When Nana plays with the Holy Rollers, they sometimes even argue over their score."

"Yes, well, life is too short, we feel, to be spent creating a game that makes one miserable rather than joyous. And golf can certainly make grown-ups miserable," Max said with a wink.

"Hey," a small voice shouted. They looked over and saw one of the house cats getting ready to tee off. "Anyone mind if I give it a whirl?"

"Go crazy!" chirped one of the cardinals.

"Don't do anything I wouldn't do," said one of the golden retrievers.

"Break a leg—I mean paw!" yelled someone else.

Adelaide and Max watched as the cat stood up on her hind legs and took a practice swing. Then she stepped up to the tee, got ready, and right before their eyes, the golf ball became exactly the right size for her. The cat swung and missed, and because she had swung with such force, she landed right on her behind. Everyone laughed and started clapping.

"Good one, Zelda!"

"Couldn't have done it better myself!"

"Hey, Zelda, I told you not to break a paw!"

Adelaide and Max laughed.

"Max, can I try?" Adelaide asked.

"My dear, of course. That's why I brought along clubs for you." He took one out and gave it to Adelaide.

"All right, everyone, Adelaide's going to have a go."

"I'm not very good at this," she said to Max as she took out her ball.

"Just do your best and be fully in the moment. Golf is a great teacher of that. Oh, and one more thing," Max said.

"Have fun?" she asked him.

"Yes indeed," he said.

Adelaide walked up to the tee and set up her ball.

"Go for it, Adelaide," said a small voice.

"You go, girl!" said another.

"Yay, Adelaide!" said a third.

Adelaide decided to just let go and, with barely any effort at all, took a swing. The ball took off into the night. Silence reigned as everyone watched. Slowly someone started to clap, then another joined, and soon all the animals were clapping and cheering. Adelaide, with a huge smile on her face, beamed at Max.

"That's the farthest I've ever hit a golf ball! What a game."

"What a game, indeed," said Max. Adelaide looked around at all the animals laughing and having a great time with the twinkling fireflies above and the full moon glowing down upon them, and she smiled. She realized that for a few moments she had completely forgotten about wanting to be grown-up. She was perfectly happy being who she was and where she was.

"And that's the beauty of the Hidden Forest," said Max thoughtfully, watching her. "We can explore it more tomorrow perhaps. There are some things I'd like to show you." He looked around at the forest, taking in the beauty of it all.

"Oh, yes!" Adelaide said

"How *wonderful* it must be!" boomed a voice suddenly. Adelaide jumped and looked around. All activity froze, and everyone looked at Max.

"It's *her*," whispered Pipsqueak. "It's the merqueen!"

"That's right. Impressive for such a pipsqueak," said the merqueen's voice.

"Max, is it really her? But I can't see her," said Adelaide.

"Unfortunately, she can see us. But she can't get to us, not here. That's what makes her so disagreeable," Max whispered.

"Ha! Enjoy yourselves now, my friends. Especially you, girl. I have my eye on you, sweetie. Oh, yes I do," said the merqueen's voice. Adelaide gulped. Then there was a huge whooshing sound and complete stillness.

"What ... what does she mean?" asked Adelaide, trying to catch her breath.

"Remember, whenever you're here, you're safe," Max said, trying to reassure her, but Adelaide could see the shadows behind his words.

"With us!" one of the cardinals chirped.

"Yeah, Adelaide, come anytime you want," said another. Max nudged Adelaide with his muzzle, and she looked around at all her new friends and felt a little better.

"But I can't stay in here forever," Adelaide said.

"That is true, my dear. But right now you're safe, and that's all that matters," Max said. "Tomorrow, then?"

"Tomorrow," Adelaide said, and tried to smile.

Chapter 10

THE HIDDEN FOREST

"THE Hidden Forest?" Louis asked after Adelaide had finished telling him all of her adventures from the night before. "You mean where all that fog is, past Nana's vegetable garden? The fog that doesn't go away?"

"Yes, and Louis, you can't believe how beautiful it is and how good you feel there. Like you could climb a million pyramids. Max said he wanted to show me some things to help with the merqueen."

"Can I come?" Louis asked.

"Well, I guess it might be okay," Adelaide said. "The question is what to tell Nana and Poppa."

"Oh, that won't be hard. Nana's on the last day

of her Holy Roller tournament, so Poppa's supposed to watch us."

"Most excellent," Adelaide said as she gave him a high five.

After Poppa had fallen asleep under the deck umbrella like clockwork, they went down to the path that led beyond Nana's vegetable garden, and into the ever-present fog.

"Max," Adelaide called gently. "I'm here! And I brought Louis too."

Through the fog, they saw Max emerging toward them, almost like a ghost coming back to life.

"Delighted to see you again. Master Louis, so glad you can join us. Follow me," he said, and led them back the way he had come. Not moment had passed, and the fog was so thick, they couldn't see their hands in front of them.

"Uh, Max…," Adelaide started. "I can't see you."

"Can you feel me though? Do you feel that I'm here with you?" asked Max.

"Yes, yes, I feel you."

"Good. Remember that feeling. It's important."

The fog grew thicker and thicker. At last it lifted, and Adelaide could see she was surrounded by gnarled bushes of gray twisted branches that tugged at her clothes as she walked.

"This is getting kind of creepy," Louis said.

Adelaide looked around at the scrub oak everywhere and couldn't help but feel the same way, although she hated admitting it. Soon they got to an impasse where all the scrub oak bushes were tangled together.

"Max, I don't think we can get through here," Adelaide said.

"Good heavens, you're not going to give up so easily, are you? I must tell you that I know you can. Most humans would stop where you are because things *looked* impassable. They wouldn't even try. But you see, if you believe you can do it, then you can. It's all just an illusion. That's what stops people ninety-nine times out of a hundred from going ahead with something. Because it *seems* impossible, so they *think* they can't continue. It's all in the mind, my dear. The ongoing battle, all up here." He tapped his paw to his head. "It's all a lot of bunk. Now, give it the old college try. Take a deep breath, back up a few steps, get a running start, and take a leap!"

"But I can't see where I'm leaping out into."

"That's it—that's the point!" Max exclaimed.

"Are you sure, Max?"

"Quite, but why don't you find out for yourself?"

"Okay. Louis, let's do it," Adelaide said as she eyed the thicket of scrub oak with uncertainty.

"Yeah!" Louis shouted. They backed up and, with Adelaide going first, ran with all their might right into it. The thicket gave way immediately, and they ran straight through. Max smiled when he heard a whoop and a holler.

"Come quick, Max!" Adelaide shouted. "You won't believe this!" Max went through effortlessly with a single leap.

On the other side, Adelaide and Louis stood in awe as they looked around. They were in a large open dell that was absolutely bursting with life. It was a brilliant green, with wildflowers of every color abounding. Birch trees covered in green moss that was almost glowing in the sunlight lined the perimeter. A duo of blue and black butterflies flitted by, followed by a much bigger moth with iridescent wings the color of moonlight. There were lovely roses climbing all around in colors of pink and ivory. Adelaide could smell bayberry, although she couldn't see where it was, and then over to her right she spotted a pine grove. On a large branch perched a family of owls, watching them.

They went through the pine grove and finally stepped into a wonderful open field with lovely tall grasses blowing in the wind. Gem-colored dragonflies chased one another overhead. It was so beautiful that Adelaide could barely believe her eyes.

"Doesn't the air smell wonderful here?" said Max as he rested in the shade.

"Yes," said Adelaide, "and I just feel so . . ."

"Alive?" said Max.

"Yes, and—"

"Not thinking about the merqueen, I bet," said Max.

"And ready to play baseball!" interjected Louis. "We could play all day in this place."

"I'll race you," said Adelaide, and she ran to a moss-covered tree for the starting point.

"You'll be sorry," said Louis as he ran over to her. He barely had time to get situated when she cried, "Go!" and took off around the field.

"Hey, no fair!" shouted Louis, but he was laughing as he tried to catch her. Adelaide finished the race at Max's spot and flopped down on the ground next to him.

"This place is so great," said Adelaide.

"And the best part about it is?" Max asked her.

Adelaide thought for a moment. "Well, I guess that I don't want to be anywhere else but right here, now." It was true. She felt the same way she had the night before; she felt okay. More than okay even, and it was such a relief.

Then, out of nowhere, a huge gust of wind blew in and patches of moss skirted away like tumbleweeds. Adelaide and Louis looked at each other, almost knowing what the other was thinking but not wanting to say it out loud.

"We'd best be getting you two home," said Max as he looked around.

"Are you looking for the watchers? Didn't Captain Henry the Twenty-Sixth say that her spies were all around?" asked Adelaide.

"I mean, how do you even know who's a spy and who isn't? It's just so complicated," said Louis.

"Yes, I'm afraid you both speak the truth. But they're not so welcome here. You see, the Hidden Forest has a very special energy that tends to keep out those who aren't pure of heart."

"How does it do that?" asked Adelaide.

"Those who aren't, shall we say, well intended get a very bad stomachache when they enter the forest. They don't know why, but they just feel awful. A very simple thing but a very powerful one as well. Onward. Adelaide, would you do us the honors?"

"I'm not sure which way though," Adelaide said, hesitating.

"Well, which way do you think? Which way *feels* right?" Max asked, watching her.

"Well," Adelaide started, looking around. "I think, maybe this way?"

"Let's give it a try, then, my dear. Forward ho!"

Adelaide led as she, Louis, and Max backtracked through the Hidden Forest. The fog became very thick once again, and the wind picked up. They could hear thunder rumbling in the distance.

"Here, now we're almost at the stone wall by your Nana's vegetable garden," said Max. "Well done, my dear. Well done indeed. Can you find your way back from here?"

"Yes, I think so," said Adelaide.

"A great adventuress like you? I'm sure you can. Now go straight in, both of you, and don't stop for anything, do you understand? Off you go, quick as you can," said Max. A huge gust of wind whooshed them toward the house as they waved good-bye.

Max watched them a moment until they got into the house. Then he looked up at the darkening sky and shuddered in the wind. With a heavy gait, he turned around and slowly made his way back along the path, disappearing into the fog.

Chapter 11

THE FAERIE FISHERMAN
AND THE UNINVITED

THE next day Poppa came home with an announcement. "Well, I've just been to Bill Fisher's, and there's no time to waste. It's just been high tide, and you know what that means."

"Bluefish?" asked Adelaide.

"Bluefish," said Poppa.

That also meant going to the beach, by the ocean, home to the merqueen. Adelaide pulled Louis aside.

"Louis, I can't go to the beach! What if . . ."

"Adelaide, are you just going to hide out forever? That's not what Amelia Earhart would have done,

I bet." Adelaide looked at him, then looked out the window, hoping for some sign, some reassurance. Louis was right. If she was going to be a great explorer someday, she had to have more courage than this. Besides, she loved being on the beach, and she loved fishing.

"Okay, I'm in," she said.

They loaded up the old turquoise Bronco and took off into the beautiful summer afternoon.

They pulled up just as a lot of the beachgoers were leaving. Poppa got out their gear and proceeded down the long boardwalk, with Adelaide and Louis close behind. Poppa took the rods out, staked them in the sand, and put on the lures. He showed them how to surf cast.

"Now, we've got to spread out. We don't want to be too close to each other, or our lines will get tangled."

Adelaide and Louis walked down the beach some but not too far in case they caught something and needed Poppa's help.

"Boy, I love this surf casting stuff," said Louis as he cast his line out into the sparkling sea.

Adelaide was feeling antsy. "I'm going to run down the beach to see if anyone else is catching anything," she said. Really she just wanted a chance to explore. Down the beach she started to go, when something caught her eye out in the water, and then there was a big splash right in front of her, like something had just landed. Was it a fish? But then it flew up out of the water like a butterfly, or a fish that had wings. She looked over at Louis to see if he saw what she was seeing, but he seemed intent on watching his fishing rod to see if there was anything on the end of it.

"Louis, look!" Adelaide exclaimed, pointing to the thing flitting around in the air. Whatever it was, it had come closer to them, and Louis was able to get a better look at it. It wasn't a fish or a butterfly but a tiny man with a long beard and a fishing pole—and wings on his back. He flew around Adelaide once very slowly, then landed on her left shoulder. Adelaide looked at Louis, speechless.

"Well, what do you know, a lass who has nothing to say! Cat got your tongue, my dear?" said the tiny man in an Irish brogue.

"Excuse me, M-Mr.?"

"Ah, bother. You don't need to be so formal, now, do you? You can just call me McFadden. That'll do just fine."

"McFadden, sir," Adelaide stammered as she

glanced over at Poppa to see if he was watching.

"Oh my darlin', you don't need to bother about him. He can't see me. Only you children can. Even if he could, he would just think he'd had too many bites of your Nana's blueberry pie."

"How did you know?"

"Acht. We know everything. You'd be surprised. Can see everything too, although that's not always such a good thing." Suddenly, a tiny pewter pint of ginger beer appeared in his hand and he drank it down happily. Louis watched him, not believing his eyes.

"Now, sir, I can see you looking at me with those peculiar eyes. And I know what you're thinking. Is this some kind of a dream? Is this the effect of delirium?" Louis's eyes widened. "Yes, my friend, I told you I know almost everything there is to know." He downed the rest of his drink and threw the pint out into the sea.

"Recycling, don'tcha know. Now, I believe you, Adelaide, want to know what exactly it is you're dealing with here. Who am I? Well, it's as you suspected. I am indeed a faerie. But I am also a fisherman, as you, Louis, may have guessed. That's right. I am a faerie fisherman! There aren't many of us left, sad to say. Especially since the merqueen has taken over. But those of us who are still around take great pride in our job. We help other fishermen, lead them to where the fish are, like I did today. I whispered in your Poppa's ear about going surf casting. Soon you'll see that he's very successful in his ventures."

Just then Poppa called out. "Hey, I got a bite! Come take a look, you two." Adelaide and Louis looked at the faerie fisherman.

"Go ahead. Take a look. I'll be right behind you. Don't worry, he can't see me. Grown-ups aren't that perceptive. They've got tunnel vision, don'tcha know."

"So, you'll tell us more about the merqueen?" asked Adelaide.

"Indeed I will. I'm afraid there's a storm brewing," he said, eyeing Adelaide.

"Adelaide and Louis, look!" Poppa yelled from down the beach as he reeled in his line.

"Go," said the faerie fisherman. "I'll just have another wee nip." He held his hand up, and another pint of ginger beer appeared in it.

"Hey, that's so cool," said Louis.

They ran over to where Poppa was. They could see the fish now, jumping out of the water. Just then McFadden appeared on Poppa's shoulder, cross-legged, drinking his pint of ginger beer.

"What a grand spectacle," McFadden said.

"Man versus Beast of the sea, fighting the good fight. I could watch all day." Adelaide and Louis quickly looked at Poppa to see if he could hear him. He couldn't, they realized in amazement.

"Ah, here you go," Poppa said as he brought the fish up onto the sand. It flopped around, and he put one foot on it and took out the hook.

"Poppa," Adelaide said as she tugged on Louis's sleeve, "we're going to go down the beach so we can catch our own fish." They ran down the beach so Poppa couldn't see them talking to the faerie fisherman.

"McFadden, we can talk now," Adelaide called. Rising out of the ocean like a tiny rocket, he reappeared and flew over to them, dripping wet.

"Had to take a dip. All that excitement gets my wee heart racing, so it does." He spun around and around in the air to get himself dry, then sat down on a piece of driftwood.

"Ay, then have a seat, lads and lasses, or lad and lass, as the case may be." Adelaide and Louis sat on the sand near him.

"Now, the first order of business is this. You'd better batten down the hatches tonight, and I mean but good. Compliments of the merqueen."

"But I put it back. I mean Max, the Sankaty

lynx, put the rose back. I'm sure he did," Adelaide said.

"Doesn't matter. The merqueen knows it was you who clipped it. You showed her a great disrespect in doing this, and she wants to teach you a lesson. If you ask me, I think she's just jealous of your two legs, when it comes right down to it. But either way, she wants you to pay."

"Oh no," Louis said as he looked at Adelaide.

"Ay. She's getting worse and worse. Way back in the beginning, you know, she was actually quite nice. Would have us all down for tea by the sea and all that. Had very funny stories to tell, so she had. But," he said with a sigh, "then it all changed."

"What happened?" asked Louis.

"Had her heart broken, so she did. By a man, too, not even a merman, but a man man, with two legs and all that. He found out she was a mermaid (she used to be able to cast a spell over herself so she had two legs instead of a tail and could come on land). Then he left her. It wasn't even because she was a mermaid. No, it was because she deceived him about who she really was. And then, to make matters worse, when she went back home to her kingdom in the sea, she was punished for misusing her power. They're not meant to cast spells on

themselves. Ever. Especially if it's to make someone fall in love with you. She was never able to go
on land again. That's why she's so sensitive about
anything that happens on land. She's especially
sensitive about her roses."

Adelaide gulped. "Well, I almost feel sorry for
her, if I weren't so afraid of her, that is," she said,
looking out to sea.

"Ay, it is a sad tale. But many creatures come
from sad tales and do not end up as spiteful as she
has. As both of you well know. But the merqueen
is a force to be reckoned with, and be sure of this:
something is on its way."

"Who told you?" asked Adelaide.

"Acht, the loud mouth frogs, of course. They
can never keep a secret. Like to brag, so they do.
They're her minions. They do her bidding on land."

"We're not safe, then. The loud mouth toads
will get us!" said Louis.

"Loud mouth frogs they are. And don't go wor-
rying about them. They don't have much power,
but they sure can trick you into thinking they do."
Just then a great breeze took them by surprise and
lifted McFadden into the air.

"Ay! Here we go," he said as he tried to keep
his balance. Then all of a sudden there was a great

whooshing, the same sound Adelaide had heard during midnight golf in the Hidden Forest when the merqueen had left. This time the sound came from the ocean. They looked out and saw the most unbelievable sight.

Rising out of the sea, perched on a giant scallop shell, was the merqueen in all her glory, glittering head to tail in jewels. Adelaide gasped and couldn't help but stare, she was so beautiful. Her violet eyes beamed at them in a most malicious manner as she casually drank from a diamond-encrusted golden goblet.

"Shark's blood, girl." She held it out to Adelaide. "Would you like some? It's really very good."

"No . . . no, no thank you." Adelaide gulped. A clap of thunder sounded overhead, though there was not a cloud in the sky.

"No? Well, well, aren't we brave to decline my invitation. How *independent*. More for me, then. More is always better. Remember that when you're grown-up, which I know you're *dying* to be." She took a long drink, then threw the goblet against a rock so that it shattered into what looked like a thousand tiny stars scattered in the sand. Adelaide could barely stay standing, her knees felt so weak.

"Here's your chance, Adelaide," whispered

RISING OUT OF THE SEA, PERCHED ON A GIANT SCALLOP
SHELL, WAS THE MERQUEEN IN ALL HER GLORY,
GLITTERING HEAD TO TAIL IN JEWELS.

McFadden. Amelia Earhart would try, Adelaide knew she would, and so would she. She stumbled forward. Louis grabbed her hand for moral support, and Adelaide was glad for it.

"Madame Merqueen," Adelaide started.

"Who?"

"Ms. Merqueen?"

"What?"

"Your Royal Highness?"

"That's more like it."

"Your Royal Highness, I understand that I've upset you by clipping your rose. But Max did put it back, and you're still angry. I'm so truly sorry, but I didn't know the rose belonged to you. If I had known it was yours, honestly, I never would have clipped it."

"Hmm. You know, I do believe you," the merqueen said with a smirk. "But it's too late. You've got what's coming to you, my sweet. For better or for worse. Now you will just have to suffer the consequences, won't you?"

"But she didn't mean it!" Louis exclaimed.

"Enough! I don't want to hear any more of this drivel!" Thunder clapped in the distance. "You know what I want," she said, glaring at Adelaide and glancing ever so casually over her legs.

"No, I-I ...," stammered Adelaide.

"Well, you'll just have to figure it out then, won't you?" With a giant swish of her tail, she flew up in the air and dove deep down into the blackening sea.

"Wait! Please!" Adelaide ran to the edge of the water, but there was nothing there. The merqueen had disappeared as suddenly as she had come.

Down the beach, Poppa called out to them holding up a bluefish and smiling. He hadn't seen a thing.

"Told you, my dears, tunnel vision," said McFadden, looking at Poppa. "Now, lass, I want you to go home and get prepared," he said as he whirled up above. "I'm going to do the same. Good luck to you!"

Adelaide and Louis ran down the beach and got to Poppa just as the rain started pelting down.

"We're off," Poppa said, gathering up their gear as quickly as he could.

For the whole drive home, Adelaide looked intently out the back window, watching.

Chapter 12

THE GIFT OF GAB

I N what seemed like the blink of an eye, the drizzle of rain turned into torrents. Adelaide, Louis, and Poppa pulled in the driveway and made it into the house just in time.

"Holy Toledo," said Poppa as he took off his gear.

"Holy Toledo for sure," said Louis as he looked out the window at the rapidly blackening sky.

"Have you ever seen a storm come on so quickly, Poppa?" asked Adelaide.

He was thoughtful for a moment before answering. "One other time, yes. Just glad to be home safe and sound."

"Yoo-hoo," called Nana from the living room. They went in and saw her kneeling down, building a fire. "I think we'll be needing this tonight."

Adelaide went to the window just as a bolt of lightning shot down from the sky. Maybe she wasn't safe even in the house. Maybe none of them were. Should they try to make it to the Hidden Forest? Did she even remember the way? she wondered as she went around locking all the windows.

"Never seen anything come on so quickly," Nana said, then paused. "Actually, that's not true. There was that one other time."

"That's what Poppa just said. What happened?" asked Adelaide.

"Someday we'll tell you," said Poppa. "When you're a little older."

"We're old now. We're old souls anyway. Isn't that what you keep telling us?" said Adelaide.

"Yeah, I'm almost, like, ten, which is like a hundred and ten in old-soul years," said Louis.

"Good try, Louis, but actually you're only eight," Adelaide said.

"So. We still want to hear the story. Please, Nana," Louis begged.

Nana hesitated. "Well, I don't know. I want you to be able to go to sleep tonight."

"We will, I promise," said Adelaide. Anything to take her mind off the merqueen.

"Hmm." Nana looked over at Poppa, who was now sitting in his favorite armchair, filling up his pipe. He gave her a wink.

"If we tell you, though," he said, "you have to promise not to tell your mother. Agreed?"

Adelaide and Louis nodded. They got comfortable around Poppa's chair by the fire as he lit his pipe. "Well, you see, it was really all your grandmother's idea," he started.

"Now, George—"

"It was and you know it. She had gotten it into her head to have a kind of séance."

"A say what?" asked Louis.

"A séance. That's when you sit in a circle and hold hands and close your eyes and ask ghosts to come for a visit, right?" Adelaide asked.

"Right you are," said Poppa, and winked at her. "We had just met, your grandmother and I, and were still just new friends. Well, she told me that she had heard talk in the town—"

"George, don't—"

"Don't worry, Del, I'm just sticking to the important stuff. As I was saying," continued Poppa, "there had been some stories going around. You see, we had been having the most unusual weather that summer. Very cold and rainy one day, then very hot, unbearably so, the next. The kind of heat you felt you could hardly breathe in. Rumor had it that a kind of curse had been put over the island. So, do you remember King Micah?"

"The Indian chief?" asked Adelaide.

"Exactly. Well, King Micah has always been very in tune with the island and its rhythms, and that particular summer he said that the weather had been so crazy because the ocean was upset."

"The ocean upset?" asked Louis.

"That's what he said. Your grandmother wasn't satisfied with that answer, so she made one of her famous blueberry pies and took it over to King Micah. Well, they talked and talked."

"One of the most fascinating conversations I've ever had," said Nana. "He told me things about Nantucket that no one would believe. Things that aren't in the science books. King Micah and his family go way back to the very beginning of when the island started."

"Well, maybe not the very beginning, since that was about ten thousand years ago," said Poppa with a chuckle.

"Details, details," said Nana.

"So, what did he tell you, Nana?" asked Adelaide. Nana looked at Poppa as he quietly smoked his pipe and gazed into the fire.

"Remember, you promised not to breathe a word of this to your mom. She'll think we've gone around the bend for sure this time," Nana said, eyeing them. Adelaide and Louis nodded.

"Well, he told me that there was a mermaid," Nana began. Adelaide gulped. "Oh yes, mermaids are real," Nana added. "There's no doubt about that. Well, this particular mermaid was very high up, a queen in fact. And she was very upset."

"The merqueen?" Adelaide asked, in almost a whisper.

"The merqueen, yes. Well, it seemed she'd had her heart broken by a man and she was going to make the whole island suffer because of it." Nana looked pointedly at Poppa, who suddenly became extremely interested in his pipe.

"Well," continued Nana, "I took it into my mind to do something about it. Maybe we could contact her and tell her how much she was affecting us. People were getting quite sick after all, with all the weather changes. I thought maybe we could be friends."

Poppa snorted. "So your Nana here," he said,

"decides to have a séance-themed cocktail party."

"It wasn't so cavalier as all that. I thought people might be more open to the idea if it seemed light-hearted," Nana explained.

"Did you invite King Micah?" asked Adelaide.

"Oh, yes. He was the most important of all," Nana said.

"Why?" asked Louis.

"Well, he believed the most fully. It was more than belief. It was a knowing," Nana said. The fire gave a loud crack, which made Adelaide and Louis jump.

"Anyone want some hot chocolate before we go on?" asked Nana.

"Yes!" said everyone at the same time, looking at one another. Nana went to put on the kettle. Poppa didn't say anything for a moment, letting all they had heard sink in. Adelaide watched the fire, and Louis watched everyone uneasily.

Finally, Nana came back, carrying a tray with four steaming mugs on it. She set it down, gave everyone a mug, and got herself comfortable.

"It was certainly a night to remember," she began.

"You can say that again," said Poppa under his breath.

"After everyone arrived, we gathered around the table and sat. King Micah told us to join hands and close our eyes. We did, and he began a sort of chant."

"An old, old Indian song," said Poppa.

"Yes. It was very beautiful actually, and as I was listening, I found myself starting to drift off, when suddenly it got very cold," Nana said.

"Oh boy, was it freezing. You could see your breath," added Poppa.

"And right as I opened my eyes, the doors, those doors right there going out to the moors, blew open with this frigid wind. King Micah said, 'She's here.'" Nana shuddered. "I've never been so scared in my life, I'll tell you."

"Who was there?" asked Louis.

"Her Royal Highness herself," said Poppa.

"The merqueen," whispered Adelaide.

"You could actually see her?" asked Louis.

"No, but you could feel her. It was her energy, her essence, if you will. Never felt anything like it before," said Nana.

"Then she spoke," said Poppa.

"Laughed is more like it. She let out this sort of cackle and said, 'Having a good summer?'"

"I almost fell back in my chair," said Poppa.

"Well, thank goodness for King Micah, who knew how to deal with her."

"So King Micah had spoken with her before?" asked Adelaide.

"Oh yes. She didn't mind him because he knew how to stay out of her way," said Nana. "He would also leave special offerings for her, because he knew how powerful she was. No, King Micah was not the one she was upset with." Nana looked pointedly at Poppa.

"Well, who then?" asked Louis.

"Me," said Poppa.

"You mean . . . ," Adelaide began.

"That's right, Addy. I'm not proud of it, but I was the man who broke her heart." Nana regarded him coolly. "It was complicated," he added.

There was an awkward silence for a moment, then Nana said, "Yes, well, that's all water under the bridge now, and well before your Poppa and I knew each other. But that summer we had a heck of a time."

"So, what did you do? How'd you work it out?" asked Adelaide.

"Compromised—made a deal," said Poppa.

"You mean *I* made a deal," said Nana. "You see, she loves our roses. Nantucket roses." Adelaide and Louis looked at each other. "Not just because they're so beautiful, but because they're so powerful. They're quite magical, you know."

"King Micah let us in on that little secret. Said the Indians knew from way back," interjected Poppa.

"They strengthen the life force," Nana said. "So we struck a deal. I felt, well, at the time I felt I was doing something for Nantucket, for the beauty of the island and for its survival. Now I'm not so sure. You see, I've grown them especially for her, beyond the stone wall there, and so far, so good. We haven't had any trouble. Every summer there's one rose in particular, a beautiful white rose, it's almost incandescent, that is the crème de la crème. The most powerful of all."

Adelaide let out a gasp. She couldn't help herself.

"What, Addy?" asked Poppa.

"Oh no," she said in barely a whisper. She looked at Louis for help, but he gulped and just stared at her.

"What is it? You look like you've seen a ghost," said Nana, going over to her.

"I-I have something to tell you," Adelaide said as she looked into the fire, trying to gather her courage.

Chapter 13

THE STORM

AFTER Adelaide finished telling her grandparents about clipping the rose, Captain Henry, Max, the Sankaty lynx, McFadden, and the merqueen, everyone was speechless. Adelaide felt like she couldn't breathe. She had been told over and over again not to go beyond that stone wall, but she had always thought it was a silly rule, not understanding the real meaning behind it. Now she realized just how very wrong she had been. If she could only relive that day and take back clipping the rose. But she couldn't; it was done now.

"Well, it's done now," said Nana, as if she had read Adelaide's mind. "And what we've got to do is figure out how to fix it." She gave Adelaide a reassuring smile, but Adelaide could see the shadows behind it. She couldn't stand it anymore.

"Oh, Nana!" She burst into tears.

Nana went over to her and gave her a hug. "Shhh, what's this? No crying. Remember, we need to stay strong. Now's the time for clear heads. We've got to do some brainstorming."

"Not to be confused with thunderstorming," said Poppa as he looked out the window at the storm. Nana shushed him. Adelaide regarded them both.

"Nana, does that mean that you and Poppa know about the Hidden Forest?" she asked.

"Yes, but we can only catch glimpses of the real Hidden Forest," said Nana.

"I can't see it at all," said Poppa, "although I know it's there. You can feel it."

"But we'd never talk about it to your mother. Her generation is far too sensible for such . . . "

"Beauty," Poppa said quietly.

"It's just that everyone seems so busy all the time," said Nana.

"Talking on cell phones," Poppa said, and shuddered. "And texting. Good heavens."

"Not really taking time to see things, the world around them," Nana added.

"Well, I'd say it's time for a little adventure," Poppa said, getting up.

"George, no," Nana said.

"Del, there's only one way to deal with the situation, and that is to face it, or face *her*, I should say."

Suddenly there was a huge flash of light followed by a tremendous crack. Then everything went black.

"Hey, cool!" said Louis.

"Don't worry, everyone, I'll get my head lamp!" Adelaide said.

"Now, wait, Addy. Let me get you a candle," Nana said as she felt her way into the kitchen. She got some candles out of a drawer, lit them, and handed one to each of them.

"George, go get the kerosene lamp," Nana said.

Holding her candle to light the way, Adelaide went into her bedroom and grabbed her head lamp from the bedside table. She wished she had brought more of her gear, she thought as she strapped it on.

"Is he really serious about going out in this, Nana?" Adelaide asked as she came back into the living room.

"You know, I actually think he is. But don't worry. He's going to have to get past me. I can play hardball when I need to, you know," she said.

Poppa came back in, carrying a lantern and his rain slicker.

"Very funny, George, but you're going out in this storm over my dead body," Nana said.

"Oh, for heaven's sake. Don't you realize that if we keep succumbing to her, it's never going to end?" Poppa said. Then he added, "I'm surprised at you, Del. Where's your sense of spirit and adventure, and your common sense?"

"You call this common sense?" said Nana.

"Heck of a lot better than hiding scared, waiting for her to come to us."

Adelaide watched them. Her heart thumped as she realized what it meant. He was going in search of the merqueen.

"I'm coming with you!" said Adelaide.

"Dear heart . . . ," began Nana.

"Addy, we've dealt with her before. We know how she is," Poppa said.

"But it's my fault this is happening. Shouldn't I be the one to fix it? Besides, it's an adventure, right?"

Poppa smiled at her. "Adelaide, you'd really be of most help if you kept an eye on things here. Delilah, keep the lantern burning, so I can find my north star again." He gave her a kiss, and with that he was gone. Adelaide watched out the window to see which path he took.

"I'm going out to the wood pile so we have enough firewood for the rest of the night," said Nana. "Get comfortable by the fire, you two, and we'll play a game when I come back. Don't worry, I know your Poppa, and he's been in worse scrapes than this." But Nana took a long glance out the window, and Adelaide knew she was worried.

When she left, Adelaide grabbed her raincoat off one of the hooks by the front door.

"Louis, you've got to stay here and look out for Nana," Adelaide said, zipping up her coat.

"No way! I'm coming with you—"

"You're only going to slow me down, and I have to catch up with Poppa!"

"I'm coming and that's it," said Louis as he frantically looked for his jacket.

"Louis, listen. The merqueen already doesn't like Nana because of what happened. We can't leave her here alone. You've got to stay. I'll be back soon with Poppa. Please, Louis."

Louis looked at her and sighed. "I miss all the good stuff," he said as he tossed his jacket onto the floor.

"Thank you," Adelaide said as she gave him a big hug. "Wish me luck."

"May the force be with you. And Poppa."

Adelaide turned her head lamp to high beam as she quickly went out the door. The rain pelted her as she raced after Poppa.

Finally she saw a light glowing in the distance.

"Poppa!" she called out. The wind was blowing so hard, she knew he wouldn't be able to hear her. Suddenly she felt a tickling by her ear.

"Lass, go ahead now. It's just a wee bit farther. He's gone to the sea, you know." It was McFadden, the faerie fisherman.

"But where?" said Adelaide as she wiped the rain from her eyes.

"Why, Polpis Harbor, of course. It's the closest one."

"Do you know the way, McFadden?" asked Adelaide.

"But of course," he said, and a tiny lantern appeared in his hand. "Just follow me, lass."

"Wait for me!" said a voice behind them. They turned to see Louis running toward them, wearing a hot-pink rain slicker that was way too big for him.

"It's Nana's rain slicker," he said, trying to

catch his breath. "Do you think she'll miss it?"

"Louis, you were supposed to stay with her," said Adelaide. "She's going to be totally worried now!"

"Nana's a grown-up. She'll be okay," Louis said.

"Hurry now, you two. We can't delay," McFadden said.

They followed him as he flitted in front of them, leading the way down an overgrown path. It started to become sandier, and they could tell they were getting closer to the beach.

"Oh boy," said Louis. "I bet the waves are really huge right now. Maybe there are giant squids and octopuses swimming around."

"What?" asked Adelaide. It was almost impossible to hear.

"Nothing!" Louis shouted.

As they went along, Adelaide kept seeing tiny red lights everywhere, flickering in the black night.

"Louis, look," she said, waving him over.

"Hey, I bet it's the loud mouth toads." He bent down to get a closer look, as did Adelaide. There, by the path, was a black creature staring up at them with glowing red eyes. It was indeed a loud mouth frog, and it flicked its extraordinarily long red tongue at them. Louis chased after it, trying to catch it, to no avail.

"They're really slippery!" he shouted to Adelaide.

"What?" she shouted back.

"Nothing!"

The frog hopped away quickly. Adelaide could have sworn she heard it giggle, although she couldn't be sure with the wind howling the way it was.

"Acht, don't be bothered about them," said McFadden. "Look!"

Up ahead they saw a twinkling glow. They heard a very faint song being sung. It was Poppa carrying his lantern and singing one of his old sea shanties. Adelaide and Louis ran to catch up with him.

"Poppa!" Adelaide shouted. "Wait!" He turned and smiled before he had a chance to catch himself. Then he became very stern and looked down on them without saying a word. Adelaide had never seen him with a look like that before.

"What are you doing?" he asked when they caught up to him, none too pleased.

"We thought you could use some help," Adelaide began.

"And you left Nana alone," Poppa said quietly. "When will you two learn? We don't have time for this now. You'll have to come with me. The sooner we deal with this, the sooner I can get home to her. Onward," he said, and continued down the path.

Adelaide looked to see if McFadden had followed them, but there was no sign of him. She heard a rustling behind them, and she moved closer to Poppa.

"What was that?" she asked.

"What?" asked Poppa.

"I thought I heard something. Did you hear that, Louis?"

"You mean like a giant landlubber *lobster* coming to get us? Yikes!" he said, and grabbed hold of Poppa's hand.

They started walking again, but after a few minutes Poppa stopped and stood listening. He turned around and looked. Adelaide and Louis did the same, but they couldn't see anything.

"Must be my imagination," he mumbled. "Okay, you two, we're almost there." They had walked a few minutes more when they began to feel the earth soften beneath their feet and smell the ocean all around them.

"Here we go," said Poppa as he led them down to the beach. "Now, you two stay here and let me do the talking." Adelaide and Louis stayed where they were as Poppa walked to the edge of the sea.

"All right, Your Highness," he shouted out to the blackness. "I know you're watching!" They waited and listened. Nothing. Then Adelaide heard some rustling. She nudged Louis, and they both turned around and let out a gasp. There were hundreds of red glowing eyes belonging to hundreds of loud mouth frogs who had crowded in behind them as far as the eye could see, blocking their way to the path. Adelaide and Louis backed up toward Poppa.

"Poppa," Adelaide said as she shook his arm.

"Adelaide, I told you—" He stumbled backward when he saw the melee of frogs. "Heavens above!" he exclaimed. A large black frog hopped forward. He wore a Nantucket Reds baseball cap with a gold crown sewn on it, and his long scarlet tongue rolled out slowly, then flicked quickly back.

"Go back!" he commanded, drooling. "Do not bother her, or you will be sorry!"

"Now, wait one minute," said Poppa, stepping forward. "We have something to say to her. Where is she?"

"It's too late! Go now! Or you and you and *you* will be sorry!" said a loud mouth frog, staring pointedly at Adelaide.

"Just who do you think you're talking to?" said Poppa. "You don't scare us, and neither does she, by the way."

Suddenly, a clap of thunder sounded, and a huge

roaring came up behind them. Just as Adelaide and Louis turned, a gigantic wave rose out of the blackness and broke over them. Louis scrambled out of it, but Adelaide could not move. It lifted her up and began pulling her out to sea.

"Poppa!" Louis shouted.

Poppa turned and grabbed Adelaide's arm, but it was as if the wave were alive, it held on to Adelaide so tightly.

Poppa struggled to pull her back in. "I've got you, Addy, and I won't let go!" With one last pull, he jerked her free of the water and onto the shore. Adelaide coughed up some water as Poppa patted her back. Louis looked from Poppa to Adelaide, when they heard another huge roar behind them.

"Go!" yelled Poppa, but it was too late. A gigantic wave crashed over them. Poppa grabbed Adelaide but couldn't reach Louis.

"Louis!" he shouted. Adelaide tried to grab Louis too, but he was already being pulled out with the waves.

"Poppa!" Louis cried, but his voice was becoming fainter. Poppa pulled off his jacket to go in after him, but a third monster wave hit them. It was all they could do to get back to the shore. Again Poppa went to go back in after Louis.

"Poppa, there's another one!" Adelaide cried. An even bigger wave than the others rose and shimmered toward them.

"I've got to try—"

"But you can't," Adelaide said, with tears streaming down her face. They could no longer see Louis. He was simply gone.

"Oh no, oh no!" Adelaide cried.

"Do you think you can make it back to the house?" Poppa asked.

"He's dead! Louis is dead."

"He's not dead, Addy. She has him. I'm sure of it. This was no accident. Come on, we've got to make a plan."

Chapter 13

THE MERQUEEN'S LAIR

L OUIS awoke with a start. He was inside a dark cave. Slowly he remembered what had happened ... the monster waves that just kept coming, being pulled away from Adelaide and Poppa out into blackness. He heard something, and looking down he saw quite a large loud mouth frog hop up to him with a silver tray balanced on his head. On it was a crystal goblet filled with a thick black liquid.

"Wow, how do you do that with—" Louis started to ask, but the frog interrupted him.

"Here's your drink," the frog said with his words drawn out and his mouth very wide.

"What is it?" asked Louis.

"Delicious and nutritious," said the frog.

"Yeah, but what is that stuff?" asked Louis again.

"Try it. You'll like it."

"No thanks. I think I actually should be going now. My family's going to be worried about me." He jumped off the slab of rock he was on but suddenly got a horrible headache. The frog started to giggle so hard that the silver tray began to fall off his head.

"Whoa!" the frog said as he grabbed hold of it.

Louis leaned against the cold stone. He felt dizzy and awful. The frog watched him for a moment with his keen red eyes, then hopped away and giggled as he held on to his silver tray. Louis watched him go. What am I going to do? he thought. How am I going to get out of here?

"You're not," said a silvery voice. He looked around, and there was the merqueen, reclining on a rock, sipping from a golden goblet.

"Want a taste?" She held her goblet out to him.

"Yeah, okay," Louis said in a daze as he went to take the goblet. Then he stopped himself. "No, no thanks actually. It might make me barf."

"Barf? How charming. What a delightful boy. Well, how do you like your new home, boy?"

"My new . . . hey, this isn't going to be my new

home. I'm going, okay? I mean if it's okay with you, I'm going to go. I'm not feeling very good."

"Maybe it's delirium," she said, winking at him. "Maybe you're going to die," she said casually as she took another sip. Louis gulped and felt like he was going to faint.

"Listen, ma'am, I'm really sorry about your rose and everything, but don't you think this is all a little too much?"

"No, I certainly do not! In fact, why don't you ask your dear Poppa about too much?"

"Okay, good idea," Louis said as he started to go.

"Nice try, but sit back down. Now—" She was interrupted when four loud mouth frogs hopped in, carrying between them a large quahog shell with writing on it.

"Your Majesty, the Oyster Report," one of the frogs announced.

"Oh yes. Goody, goody, goody," she said as she snatched the shell from them and looked it over. Her eyes began to glow a most brilliant violet, and a smile spread across her face. "Well, isn't this just divine. Six hundred and thirty-nine more pearls have been found. All for me. How wonderful." She took the shell and threw it against the ground so that it shattered. "We don't want it to fall into the wrong hands now, do we?" She signaled the frogs to go with a wave of her hand and snapped, "Leave us!" They bowed and hopped backward out of the room.

"Now, where were we?" she asked Louis absently. "Oh yes, we were talking about the girl."

"The girl?" Louis asked. "You mean Adelaide?"

"Yes, Adelaide. What a lovely name. For a thief."

"She's not a thief. She made a mistake that anyone could have made," Louis said, forgetting he was scared for a moment.

"Well, now she's got to pay the piper. I have a little deal to make with her. I want her. Here. Now! And you're going to help me with that."

"No, I'm not," said Louis. He'd had about enough of this whole thing. The merqueen was beautiful all right, but he didn't feel well around her. Not only that, but a smell he couldn't put his finger on was beginning to linger in the air. A smell very much like the old bird skeletons he used to collect. It was the smell of decay.

"No," he continued. "Never in a million years." The merqueen laughed, and her violet eyes gleamed at him very brightly.

"Charming, just charming. Don't you see? It's

too late. You've already helped, because you're here. Oh yes, without even meaning to, you've helped to lure her here."

"What, me? No, she wouldn't—" Louis stopped short and realized with a horrible chill that the merqueen was right. Adelaide would come looking for him, wherever he was, if she thought he was in trouble.

"Oh no," said Louis quietly to himself.

"Oh yes," said the merqueen, grinning.

Chapter 14

KING MICAH

A DELAIDE, wearing her leather flight jacket for good luck, took hold of Nana's hand as she, Nana, and Poppa walked quickly down the dirt road to King Micah's cottage. The sun was just coming up, but it was much cooler since the storm had passed, which it did almost immediately after Louis was taken. Tears pricked Adelaide's eyes when she thought of it all, but she quickly brushed them away. There was work to be done. When she and Poppa had gotten home and told Nana what had happened, Nana said there was only one person who'd be able to help, and that was King Micah.

Adelaide had butterflies in her stomach and her mouth was dry as they made their way down the path. Maybe King Micah would say that it was all her fault for being too adventurous, and there was nothing he could do now. All she knew was that she really missed her brother.

"We're almost there," said Nana, and gave her hand a squeeze. Adelaide looked apprehensively at her.

"Don't worry. I think you're going to like him," Poppa reassured her.

"He must be really old now," said Adelaide.

"Yes, I'd say so."

"How old do you think he is, Nana?"

"No one really knows for sure," said Nana. "Look, there it is." Adelaide saw a gray shingled cottage at the end of a large open field overlooking the sea. It was very much in keeping with most of the houses she saw on Nantucket, and yet there was something different as well. As soon as they entered the field she felt a shift, but nothing she could really put her finger on.

When they came up to the house, the sea-green wooden door opened and out came one of the tallest men Adelaide had ever seen. He had hair the color of smoke, tied back in a long ponytail. His skin was as dark as the pine trees next to him and had so many wrinkles and deep crevices, it reminded her of bark. He looked at them with great warmth in his eyes but no smile, no greeting. Adelaide liked him immediately. The butterflies in her stomach were gone.

"Well," King Micah finally said as he gazed at Adelaide. "I was told that you would be coming."

"That I would be coming?" Adelaide echoed.

"Well, I'm not talking to the scrub oak, now, am I?" he said. Nana smiled at him as she squeezed Adelaide's hand in comfort.

"Hello, Delilah," he said. "Not very surprised that you're in the middle of things once again."

"King Micah," Nana said, nodding. "And I'm not surprised that you're the one we've come to for help once again."

"No, neither am I," he said with a sigh as he motioned for them to come into the cottage.

Inside, it was as if they had wandered into another realm. The air was very cool and smelled of sage and lavender. It was quite dark, but there was movement all around. As Adelaide's eyes adjusted, she saw what was causing the activity. Everywhere she looked there were animals.

In one corner a small fawn nestled on a bed

of pine needles. One of its legs was wrapped up in bandages. Up above, a tiny owl was moving back and forth on its perch as it watched them. On wooden chairs by a table, two black cats were curled up together. The fawn looked up at her.

"Can I?" Adelaide asked as she bent down to pet it.

"Ask her," said King Micah.

"Can she talk?"

"No, Adelaide, we're not in the Hidden Forest here, but humans can communicate with animals in the everyday world. Look, hold out your hand for her to smell," said King Micah. Adelaide held out her hand as she slowly sat next to the fawn to pet her. Suddenly she felt overwhelmed by all that had happened, and tears started to roll down her face.

"King Micah, I ...," she started but was completely at a loss for words.

"I know you're worried, Adelaide, and I know you think it's all your fault," King Micah said gently.

"But—" Adelaide started.

"Hold on there. This was all meant to happen, you see. Things could not continue as they have been with the merqueen. The fact is, Adelaide, you are our catalyst—we have only to thank you."

"To thank me?"

"Oh yes. She's been holding forth on this island for so long, controlling things that shouldn't be in the control of anyone but nature. So many different creatures living in fear for too long now. It's a relief that this is all happening. It's time to face her. That's all."

"Adelaide," said Poppa, "tell King Micah what happened."

"Well, King Micah, I did face her."

"Did you? What happened?"

"I don't really understand for sure. She said I know what she wants. The thing that would make it all better. She wants me to give her this thing. I just need to figure out what it is, so we can get Louis back."

King Micah and Nana looked at each other.

"I'm afraid what she wants, this one and only thing, you simply aren't able to give her," said Nana, putting her arm around Adelaide.

"Why not? What does she want?"

King Micah finally spoke. "She wants to be human, Adelaide."

"You mean . . ."

"You would trade places with her. You would have to become a mermaid," Nana said. "Don't worry dear. It simply won't happen."

"Is it possible, though?" Adelaide asked quickly.

King Micah and Nana looked at each other. "Then Louis would be safe, wouldn't he?" asked Adelaide. They didn't answer her. Suddenly Adelaide grew very hot and felt like she couldn't breathe. She needed air. She needed to be alone. She reached for the door.

"Addy...," Nana started, but Adelaide was already out the door before she could finish.

"Let her go," said King Micah quietly.

Adelaide ran out of King Micah's cottage and didn't look back. She didn't know where she was going, but she knew she needed to just keep putting one foot in front of the other.

Chapter 15

ALL FOR ONE

ADELAIDE ran down the path that led away from King Micah's cottage into the woods. It was cooler out now, and she ran as fast as she could, tears streaming down her face. Soon she came to a fairly thick area in the woods where the path she was on disappeared and it wasn't clear which way to go.

"Oh no," she said out loud, even though she was alone.

"Don't worry, girlie." She looked down, and there was Captain Henry the Twenty-Sixth, the mouse she had met when all of this had started, when she had clipped the merqueen's rose. But wait, hadn't he gone over to the other side? Not only that, but he looked horrible. His head was bandaged with a bloody white rag, and he had a black patch over one eye. It looked like he was missing an ear.

"Captain Henry," Adelaide said. "Are you all right?"

"What's a girlie like you doing in a place like this?"

"I was, I was just running," Adelaide said, gathering her courage.

"Just running, just clipping a rose. You think you're so innocent, don'tcha?"

"Isn't she though?" said a voice from behind Adelaide. Out walked Max, the Sankaty lynx, with McFadden, the faerie fisherman, sitting on his back.

"Ay, you can say that again," said McFadden.

Adelaide couldn't have been happier to see them. "McFadden! Max! Where'd you come from?"

"You're almost in the Hidden Forest now, my dear," said Max. "You're in our neck of the woods," he said, looking pointedly at Captain Henry the Twenty-Sixth.

"Tsk," said Captain Henry as he took off his gold helmet and rubbed the red ruby in the center. "That's right, I'm just passing through. Don't worry, wouldn't want to trespass in your precious forest. But I'll tell you this, missy. She means what she says and says what she means, got it?"

"A translation, if you please," said McFadden.

"You heard me, fatso," he said, and with one jump disappeared into the undergrowth.

"Fatso!" said McFadden.

"I don't feel well when he's around," said Adelaide.

"That's a lesson, isn't it? Always listen to your gut," said Max. "And remember, Adelaide, you're never alone."

"Certainly not," said a small voice.

"Absolutely no way," said another.

"We're with you, Adelaide," said a third. She turned to see animals coming from all directions. Some of them she recognized from midnight golf, like Fredrick, the house cat with the plaid beret, and the bright red cardinals that flitted around the birch branches overhead. Zelda, another house cat, approached them as well, accompanied by two golden retrievers. Three rabbits she had never seen before appeared from under some scrub oak.

"They're the Murphy brothers," said Max. "They're very fast."

Adelaide heard a twig snap behind her and saw two beautiful deer approach. One was the small fawn that was at King Micah's cottage with its leg bandaged. Adelaide looked around at all these wonderful creatures and felt a wave of gratitude.

"So you see, my dear, there's nothing to fear but—" Max started saying.

"ME!" boomed an unmistakable voice. At the sound of the merqueen, most of the animals scattered instantly, a natural reaction to such a fearsome noise. Adelaide grabbed hold of Max as he looked up to the sky, but there was nothing to be seen.

"I know it seems she's here, but she's not," Max reassured Adelaide.

"Are you really so sure of that?" asked McFadden strangely. It almost looked as if he was smirking at Adelaide.

"McFadden. . . ," she started, when there was a tremendous trembling of the earth.

"Ah yes. That would be the ocean tides getting ready to make their way inland," said the merqueen's voice. "Mr. McFadden, you can take your leave now. And I thank you from the bottom of my, uh, what is that pesky thing called? Oh yes, my heart."

McFadden bowed very deeply, as if to the heavens. Adelaide gasped, and all the color drained from Max's muzzle as he reached back with his paw to feel for the earth, for he had to sit to take this all in.

"It can't be true," Max said as he stared at McFadden.

"Don't be such a sentimental old cat," McFadden said. "Oh, and I should tell you, Max, grand master poobah Sankaty lynx, that I'm surprised at you, very surprised. Things must stay the same so we can all remain safe and sound. There must be some kind of order maintained. You should know that, you really should."

Max looked as if he were in a daze, and Adelaide went over to him and took his paw.

"It's going to be okay, Max. I'll make sure of it, I promise you."

"Beware of those who are the most charming and quick to be your lifelong friend, for they are the ones who can be most treacherous," Max said in a whisper.

"How touching!" boomed the merqueen's voice. "But if the girl is to make things right, then what is she still doing here? Time is of the essence, my darling girl. For your precious Nantucket and

ADELAIDE LOOKED UP TO THE SKY. "TELL ME WHAT
YOU WANT!"

especially for your dear brother. Who knows how much longer the boy will last? Who's to say?"

"This is the perfect moment to exit stage left," said McFadden as he flitted higher into the sky. "After all, when the going gets tough, the tiny better get going, don't you know? Looks like the high tide's going to be a wee bit earlier than expected! And I know how much cats love the water." With that he spun off and away, like a leaf in the wind.

Adelaide looked up to the sky. "Tell me what you want! Anything you want and I'll do it!" she shouted to the merqueen.

"We will trade our essences, you and I. I will be free to walk among humans, free to love and be loved. You will have a wondrous kingdom down below. You will be a queen! There are many adventures to be had, my dear, many thrilling escapades. Then the boy will be safe once more."

"But my family, will I ever see them again?"

"Of course. You will be able to see them. From afar. You just won't be able to be with them. Many things will be yours, many beautiful things. You will be a queen! Come now, let it be done!"

There was a great swooshing sound and then silence. The merqueen's energy left as quickly as it had come.

"Right. A plan, we need a plan," said Max, gathering his strength and getting back on his paws.

"A plan?" said Pipsqueak. "We all know what she wants. Adelaide and her legs. That's what she wants. *And* we all know she's not going to stop until she gets what she wants."

"He's right," said Adelaide. "We could all fight her, of course we could, and a lot of you would get hurt or worse, and in the end, she still wouldn't have what she wants, which is me. So you see," she said, looking around at their shining faces so full of urgency, "I have to go, and I have to go alone." Adelaide didn't want to cry at this moment. She wanted to be like Amelia Earhart, who looked danger in the face and flew right into it. She didn't want them to see how very scared she was.

"I can't wait any longer. I have to go."

"Then we'll go with you, Adelaide," said one of the Murphy brother rabbits.

Max watched her a moment and said, "We'll all go."

"For moral support!" chirped one of the cardinals.

As the wind began to whip around them, they all set out. Adelaide's thoughts ran over all the plans she had made, exotic places around the world she would discover and explore. Now all that was not to be. Even so, she felt compelled and she knew what she had to do. She began to run, and all the animals followed.

Through the Hidden Forest they went. Through the silvery branches of the birch trees, through the vibrant rosebushes that made her feel as though she could do anything, and slowly her courage grew. Even though the fog was thick around them, somehow she knew where to go.

Finally they got to the path by King Micah's cottage that led out to the vast, open sea. Down through the sand dunes Adelaide went, with Max following, right down to the ocean's edge. Rain was coming down in pellets now, and it was hard to see. Adelaide looked out at the massive waves breaking in the distance. She took a deep breath and shouted out, "Your Highness, I accept!"

"Oh goody!" boomed the merqueen's voice out of nowhere, and a huge wave came up, then crashed down on Adelaide. She completely lost her footing and felt the tide pulling her out to sea.

"Hold on, Adelaide," called Max. "It will bring you back in again." He was right. The wave lifted her up and dropped her right back on the beach where she had been.

"Oh, Max, I'm scared. I don't want to live under the sea, even if it means I'm going to be a queen."

"Now, Adelaide, you're going to have to trust me. You're going to have to listen to what I say and do it, even if it seems like it doesn't make any sense at all, all right?"

"Okay, Max. I trust you."

"All right. Now shout out to the merqueen that you're ready, like you just did, but say that you want to see Louis first, so you know he really is safe. Go ahead."

Adelaide cupped her hands around her mouth and shouted out to the ocean, "Your Highness, I'm ready, but I won't go anywhere until I see that Louis is safe and you're keeping your side of the bargain!" In a whisper she said to Max, "Was that okay?"

"That was just fine," he said, and nudged her with his muzzle.

A clap of thunder sounded and a gust of wind blew Adelaide backward, making her stumble on the sand. Then she heard a small voice.

"Hey, this is kind of cool!" It was Louis. Adelaide wiped the rain from her eyes, and off in the distance she could make him out. He was sitting on top of a giant clamshell that was being pushed along by a dozen loud mouth frogs. Adelaide jumped up and down and hugged Max, she was so happy to see Louis.

"Louis!" She waved at him. At that moment she knew she was doing the right thing. "Max, what next?"

"Go tell her you're ready. Go now!" Adelaide hugged Max again and looked back at some of the animals that were now watching her from the forest, cheering her on. She ran forward to the edge of the ocean and shouted, "I'm ready!"

A huge bubbling rose up in the water beside Louis. Then the merqueen appeared, all in sparkling white, as if dressed for her own wedding. Louis saw her and slowly tried to edge over to the side of the giant shell so he could jump into the ocean. He didn't want to have anything more to do with her.

"Not so fast," she said, her violet eyes glaring at him. "Girl, prepare yourself!"

Adelaide looked at the merqueen, then at Louis.

"I'm ready," she said, almost in a whisper.

"*Most excellent.*" The merqueen cackled as she raised both her arms to the heavens and a tremendous bolt of lightning shot down. Then it seemed as though everything happened at once. As if in a dream, Adelaide saw Max leap in front of her, blocking her as she was completely blinded and blown backward by a huge force of energy. Then a roar came upon them, almost like a beast, swooping around and zooming away off into the distance. A low rumbling followed it, then complete silence. The wind and the rain had completely stopped, as if turned off by a switch. Adelaide opened her eyes, and who was right beside her but Louis, grabbing onto the giant clamshell for dear life. The sea was completely calm, and the merqueen was nowhere in sight.

"Louis!" She gave him a big hug, and this time he didn't squirm away. "But where's Max?" Suddenly she gasped as she looked down, for there was Max lying at her feet.

"Max!" She got down beside him and took his paw. Louis knelt down beside her. "Max, can you hear me? Please tell me you can hear me."

Max slowly opened his eyes and looked at her. "She's left, my dear. Gone for good, I should think." But then he closed his eyes again and his breathing halted.

"Max, please, no . . . ," Adelaide whispered.

"Shh. Now listen to me, Adelaide. You're on your way to being a grown lady because you've made the choice to sacrifice for the sake of someone else. You've broken her spell because your intention was completely pure and selfless. You were willing to give up the one thing that meant the most to you for the one person who meant the most to you. That kind of love is the only thing that could do it. You've truly opened your heart, and because of that you will be able to experience more joy than an ordinary grown-up. If you don't let yourself experience great sorrow, then you will never feel great joy. The two go hand in hand, my dear. You're now extraordinary, and don't ever forget it."

Max stopped and was quiet a moment. Adelaide wiped sand from his muzzle. "Max, please don't go..."

Max opened his eyes and watched them both. He smiled. "It's the way, my dear. But promise me one thing. That you'll never forget the Hidden Forest. It's here always." And with great effort he lifted his paw and placed it on Adelaide's heart. "Here," he said, and closed his eyes for the last time. Adelaide started to weep so hard that Louis didn't know what to do to comfort her. Finally Louis felt a hand on his shoulder. It was King Micah, who carefully led him away.

"Max was right," King Micah said as he observed Adelaide from a distance. "It is the way. Let her have her time. It will ebb and flow, her grief. Like the tides. That is as it should be." Then King Micah held out his hand to Louis, and together they walked slowly up the sandy path back to his cottage, where Nana and Poppa were waiting for them.

Adelaide stayed with Max until the sun started to set. Then she slowly took off her flight jacket and laid it over him. The Murphy brothers quietly came down and gently carried Max away. Adelaide looked out to the sea and watched the scarlet horizon, then turned away and slowly walked back up the path.

Chapter 16

ROSA RUGOSA

EEKS later, after Adelaide had finished packing up to go home, she meandered down the path by the stone wall to bid adieu to the Hidden Forest. She smiled to herself, thinking that's something Max would have said. It was a lovely day, and Adelaide's pace was slow as she took in everything around her. It was really such a beautiful place, Nantucket. How lucky she was to be able to come here, how lucky.

She watched the wind rustling the birch trees and seagulls flying overhead on their way to find some crabs on Jetties Beach. She got a waft of some rosa rugosa bushes and bent down to smell them when she saw a rustling behind one. A tuft of fur appeared, then out walked the spitting image of Max the Sankaty lynx, but with a black silk scarf tied around her neck rather than the green cravat Max had worn in what seemed like a lifetime ago. Adelaide gasped.

"My dear," the lynx said. "I feel like I know you already from everything Max told me."

"Everything Max told you? Are you . . ."

"Mrs. Max, my dear, and it's a great honor to make your acquaintance." Mrs. Max held out her paw to Adelaide, who took it most gingerly and gave it a little shake. How that paw reminded her of Max.

"Mrs. Max, I'm so sorry."

"I know you are, my dear, but please believe that I know it was the way, and so I don't blame you, not one bit. Max would have wanted us to feel that way, you know. So without further adieu, may I introduce to you . . ." She paused and looked back into the rosebush.

"Maxine! Maximillius! Come out here, please."

From behind the roses, two Sankaty lynx kittens shyly walked out. They were the spitting image of Max as well, and each had a black silk scarf tied around the neck, in mourning for their father. Adelaide bent down and shook their paws very carefully and told them how happy she was to make their acquaintance.

"But how is it that I never knew about you?" Adelaide asked Mrs. Max.

"Well, Max didn't like to mix his work with his private life, you see."

"His work?"

"Yes, of course," Mrs. Max said with a smile. "His work was you, my dear girl."

"What do you mean?"

"You are the first, you see. To be let into our world fully. It was time for our two worlds to come together. Overdue, really. Max was so pleased, Adelaide, very proud of you indeed . . . " Mrs. Max couldn't continue. Her voice broke, and Adelaide knew how upset she was, though trying not to show it. She gently took Mrs. Max's paw and said quietly, "It's okay, I know, and I'm so sorry, Mrs. Max. I miss him too. I really miss him." Mrs. Max couldn't hold back, and she let herself weep, fully and completely. Adelaide held her, and so did Maxine and Maximillius, silently supporting her.

Finally Mrs. Max took out a handkerchief with the initials MSL embroidered on it and wiped her eyes.

"But life goes on, my dear. It's what my Max always said, and it's true. Here, he wanted you to have this."

Mrs. Max went behind the rosebush and came out holding something in her mouth. It was the merqueen's rose, dried and preserved perfectly. Mrs. Max gently laid it at Adelaide's feet. Adelaide picked it up.

"So he never did put it back," Adelaide said.

"No, it would have been the absolutely wrong thing to do. Then things would have gone on the same forever—with her calling the shots. You see, no one before you had had the courage, or shall I say gumption, to get the rose. Gumption, which turned into courage. We really are so grateful to you, my dear."

Adelaide and Louis stood by the railing on the top deck of the ferry and waved to Nana and Poppa as it started to back out of the slip. Adelaide couldn't believe it was already time to go home—it seemed like just a moment ago they were pulling into Nantucket Harbor.

The ferry pulled around slowly and headed out to sea. Adelaide buttoned up her cardigan sweater and put her arm around Louis as they went by the

Brant Point Lighthouse. Adelaide took two pennies from her pocket and gave Louis one; they threw them into the harbor, each silently making a wish. Fall was on its way, and that meant school would start again, and so would everything else that was part of their ordinary life. Not ordinary anymore, thought Adelaide. She reached into her pocket again and pulled out a small bundle wrapped in tissue. It was the rose that Max had kept for her. She smiled and inhaled deeply. How she loved the smell of roses.

CPSIA information can be obtained at www.ICGtesting.com
Printed in the USA
LVOW02*2357180515

438988LV00007B/7/P